Newcastle
Short Story Award

HUNTER
WRITERS
CENTRE

First published in Australia in 2022 by Hunter Writers Centre
www.hunterwriterscentre.org
Newcastle Short Story Award Anthology 2022
ISBN 978-0-6453756-2-6

Cover photograph by
Brendan Somerville & licenced through iStock

Published by Hunter Writers Centre Inc. 2022

Hunter Writers Centre
Newcastle NSW 2300

hunterwriterscentre.org

HUNTER
WRITERS
CENTRE

Judges' report

From Joey Bui and Bram Presser

As readers, we can't help wondering about our writers. We want to know what their lives are like, and whether they experienced what their characters did. But that's not really what fiction tells us. Fiction tells us what the writer's imagination is like and what she can conjure. And it's a gift when fiction can take us into an imagination unlike our own and expand us. That's what the prize-winning stories did this year, each in their own way.

First Prize: Stop Motion
From its wonderfully absurd opening line, we knew we had stumbled upon something special. Bold, unsettling and often hilarious, *Stop Motion* offers a glimpse into the Quixotic dreams we all pursue, juxtaposed against the often-crushing realities of everyday life. The unnamed narrator would fit among literature's great hopeless misfits. He charms and exasperates the reader in equal measure. Whether in his morally suspect day job writing obituaries for corporate elites or his passion project filming a stop motion Lego adaptation of Dostoevsky's masterpiece, *The Brothers Karamazov*, we can't help but root for what we, as readers, know is an impossible ending. When a conclusion of sorts does come, there is little else to do than shake our heads and laugh. Every line shimmers with insight and heart, and not a word is wasted. *Stop Motion* is a superb story and a very worthy winner.

Second Prize: Gabby in Bed
Gabby in Bed is expertly tense. The characters are original and persuasive. The dialogue surprises, while deftly tracking the many layers of power and desperation at play between a woman and her estranged mother. Each character has an estimation of herself and the other, each is trying to project a persona to the other, and each trying to make the other feel a certain way. Then there are the precisely placed details that contain worlds—Gabby moves around her cluttered room, 'leaning on things every so often, with a sure sense of what would hold her and what would give way.' It's a rare story devoted to making a case for each of its competing characters; they are alive and straining against bias, ego, and expectation.

Third Prize: The Sins of Coal Ridge

This is a story we want to (and have) read again and again. The mining town of Coal Ridge is fully-realised. The prose is comprehensive yet tight, and edged with a sly narration that feeds into the story's atmosphere of shame and desperation. 'Bloated wombats litter the roadside.' Our main character smokes from a 'pipe as big as a sheep's horn,' and a woman's hair is redder than Australian flame trees. Incredibly, each of the story's fifteen characters are vividly painted—we can see each of them beyond the pages of this story, anxious to get what they want, and trying to forget their ugliness.

Congratulations to all the winners, and every author whose wonderful story is published in this collection. We have no doubt that you will delight in these pages as much as we did.

Joey Bui and Bram Presser

1st Prize donated by The University of Newcastle
Stop Motion - Benjamin Hickey

2nd Prize donated by Westfield Kotara
Gabby in Bed - Finegan Kruckemeyer

3rd Prize donated by Hunter Writers Centre
The Sins of Coal Ridge - A.J. Henry

Highly Commended donated by Officeworks Kotara
Good Shoes - Andrea Rowe

Commended donated by Foghorn Brewhouse
The Bendigo Marxist Ladies' Auxiliary - Amanda Hildebrandt

Commended donated by Hunter Writers Centre
After - Darcy-Lee Tindale

Local Award donated by Macquariedale Organic Wines
The Waves - Glenn Stuart Beatty

Local Award donated by Pepper Tree Wines
Pigboy on the Train - Shea J Evans

Local Award donated by Tulloch Wines
Earthquake Correspondents - Garry Jennings

Local Award donated by Tamburlaine Organic Wines
Cosmic Latte - Michael Tippett

Contents

Judges' report   iii

Stop Motion   9
Benjamin Hickey

Gabby in Bed   15
Finegan Kruckemeyer

The Sins of Coal Ridge   21
A.J. Henry

Good Shoes   25
Andrea Rowe

The Bendigo Marxist Ladies' Auxiliary   31
Amanda Hildebrandt

After   37
Darcy-Lee Tindale

The Waves   45
Glenn Stuart Beatty

Pigboy on the Train   51
Shea J Evans

Earthquake Correspondents   57
Garry Jennings

Cosmic Latte   65
Michael Tippett

Chrysalis: the aftermath   72
Michelle Haines Thomas

The Bonfire   76
Kate Murdoch

Dead Dreams   81
Sandeep Kumar Mishra

The Birdwatcher   87
Christine Johnson

Homecoming   93
James Noonan

Down into the Hellhole   98
Jim Brigginshaw

Eleven-Thirty   103
Sally Jane Smith

Rest & Recuperation 107
Sinead Reilly

Friday 111
Rosanne Dingli

The Colonel 116
Vito Milana

Get it off Your Chest 122
Tyler Heesh

The Bone Pearl 128
Keshe Chow

Hermit's Hut 134
Kerry Munnery

Too Much and Not Enough 139
Kathryn Goldie

Lost at Sea 144
Martin Watson

Girl 149
Keren Heenan

My Cousin Has Bought a Metal Detector 154
Catherine Moffat

Superman 159
Dan Davies

Opal 163
Michael Mueller

Burial of a Dream 166
Jim Brigginshaw

The Visit 172
Morna Seres

Roundabout 178
Lisa Kate Moule

Wonder Lost 184
Regina Botros

Stop Motion

Benjamin Hickey

1st Prize

I am remotely employed to write the obituaries of semi-prominent shareholders of the least unethical of the four big banks for a bi-monthly internal publication. My primary task is to maintain a safeish position in the evanescent nexus of the Team's alliances.

The document on my laptop screen in my office-studio—the second of two bedrooms in my rented ninth-storey flat—contains the same seven words it did four hours ago:

Donald Ronald Edward AO, 1933-2022, Nickel-Sector Elder Statesman

I lie face down on the off-white carpet and enjoy the smell of dust.

After work, I work on my film, a stop-motion animation of *The Brothers Karamazov* I am making out of Lego. We have, at most, one truly great idea, and if I do, this is mine: an explosive synthesis of high and low culture which detonates post-Christian teleologies of hope in the anthropocene. As well as the most sophisticated and accessible adaptation of the novel to date, it will blast me free from obits forever.

I'm under no illusions about the dearth of professional stop-motion animation opportunities in Australia—the industry has suffered from funding cuts and dwindling engagement. But I've been working on the film since I finished my screenwriting masters ten years ago. I have to believe there's a chance I'll make it big.

I am working on the scene where Ivan meets the devil. All art is intertextual, and I paint with a rich palette of sources. The coal shovel is from the 1998 Dolphin Windsurfer kit, the goblet is from 2001 Hagrid's Hut and the cushions are panels of the Millennium Falcon.

The limitations of my medium insist that difficult decisions must be made. For instance, is it more important that the bricks of the walls more closely resemble the scale of those in typical mid-nineteenth century Muscovite dwellings, or the pattern of their construction? I tell myself that these compromises are expressions, not betrayals, of my commitment to verisimilitude.

And while I've sworn to use only Lego for the structures and humans, I've allowed myself the luxury of making the finer furnishings from other materials: hand-sewn linen curtains no bigger than fingernails; lightable candles with wicks of my hair; a custom-printed bible, in readable Cyrillic, the size of a chip of tooth.

When Ivan and the devil are in place, I set up my tripod. The key is to move the pieces so subtly—the twist of a yellow c-shaped hand, the turn of a little head—that the naked eye cannot detect the difference between each frame. I take the first photo, but the lighting is wrong. It's wrong on the next one too. After twenty-five twitches of the lamp I realise the set dining room table is absurdly tall: halfway up the standing Ivan's chest. This would distract any viewer from the dialogue, which I am nowhere near ready to even think about recording. I inspect the set closer, have a head spin and throw everything back in the drawer.

Seven years ago I saw a stop-motion animated advertisement for cold and flu medication. It was shoddy work—the butterfly's wings flapped with staccato violence. Clay is not my medium, but I plucked up the courage to write to the pharmaceutical company explaining their mistakes. They never got back to me, but it was good to get my name out there.

Richard Abel Albright AO, 1938-2022, Former Victorian Minister for Racing

I meet my friends on Zoom for our perpetual online Monopoly game. Our house rules make it impossible to lose: you just keep paying rent and accruing debt. We spend the night clarifying, debating and arguing the intricacies of the rules until someone gets upset. Each of us have a series of spreadsheets to determine the optimum decision for each particular circumstance. I leave each session drunk, with a private resolve to never play again.

At night, to get to sleep, I add up the costs of houses and properties, the odds of going to jail on your third roll from GO!, or the median benefit of Community Chest. When I can no longer hold onto the figures, I know I'm on the edge of cosy darkness.

After my girlfriend left—a reasonable decision—I slept with a mother of two I met on a stop-motion animator dating site. I fucked her in her Mr Whippy van, among jars of stale peanuts and metal tins of hundreds of thousands. She seemed grateful and I felt proud, but we haven't spoken since.

I am trying to determine the rate of my hairline's retreat. Each year, in June, I take a photo of my forehead with my laptop's inbuilt camera. Then I compare the images, like maps of the Arctic Ice.

I was twelve when the Gatorade people came. The class sat cross-legged on the scuffed basketball court while they gave a special lesson about electrolytes. She had a ponytail and he had frosted tips. Grateful to miss the ritualised humiliation of regular double P.E., I read and re-read the gold-leaf names of School Captains past on the wooden boards high on the walls.

'We're so pumped to tell you guys about the Hydration Education Challenge!' the Gatorade man said. 'Thousands of students in hundreds of schools all around Australia are making one-minute videos about why fluids matter. The winner will get $500 for themselves and $5000 for your school, all thanks to one of Australia's most high-powered sports drinks!'

A hated girl put up her hand. 'Isn't it healthier just to drink water?'

He flinched and said: 'It's no worse than cordial.'

I remember the whites of the Gatorade woman's eyes. 'Who's thirsty?' She screamed. 'Who's thirsty?!'

We all lined up for styrofoam cups half-filled with orange or blue.

I was building a garden with Lego on my bed when Mum came in with tears on her cheeks and the phone in her hand.

'Your animation won,' she said.

The honey light that oozed through the window had a quality I've never seen since.

The Principal's office smelt of new cars and cologne. I still remember the things on the wall: the Principal with the local MP, the Principal with his family at the Alps, a reproduction of Da Vinci's *The Last Supper* and a clipping of the article. My face was made of minute black dots, like the nodules on a Lego brick.

'Some students—some people—have what we might call a gift. This won't be the last time I see your photo in the newspaper.'

I take my mother to an apple orchard outside Geelong.

'I know they won't have it,' she says in the car, little hands clasping her bag. 'It's a wild goose chase.'

The radio drools syrupy pop. I can't be bothered turning it off.

'Like that poem by Mary Baker Eddy. No, she was the Christian Science woman, wasn't she? When my grandmother got pneumonia—'

'You've told me this story.'

Raised in Melbourne's eastern suburbs, which stretch to eternity, mall by mall, I am always shocked by the blankness of the west. Dead dry field follows dead dry field, foreshadowing the desert. Did something graze here? Was it once bush? I don't care enough to find out.

'They won't have it. It's like I like to be disappointed.'

Shock jocks laugh like jackals as we pass a new estate. Yardless, eaveless houses huddle: penguins on an ice-shelf.

'Awful,' Mum murmurs. 'Why would anyone live here?'

We argue about negative gearing then settle into a comfortable tension. Should I sell Trafalgar Square? I total up the numbers.

'Thank you for finally taking me out here,' she says. 'I know how busy you are.'

She hasn't driven for three years, since a fourteen-wheeler totalled her lilac Mazda and right shoulder at an intersection near the Kmart where she worked. The driver had been awake for 72 hours, chewing his daughter's Ritalin to Brisbane and back to pay for her upcoming school fees. On the dock, he sobbed about his divorce, pawing his bald scalp as if to find comfort from a softness that was no longer there.

It was around then that Mum started on the apples.

As a girl, she and her three older brothers (now estranged, dead, and living in Canberra, respectively) rode ponies and picked wildflowers on their father's pig farm. An Elysian field at the property's rear contained a single tree. The kids sat under its wrinkled boughs and ate the gifts it dropped them: the subtlest, sharpest, sweetest, smoothest fruit on earth. She's sure it was some rare heirloom breed, but hasn't tasted it in the half-century since it was bulldozed for a highway. I wonder if the skulls of pigs are still beneath the bitumen. Now she goes from orchard to orchard, craving another hit.

I spot the misspelled cardboard sign on the side of the dusty road:

Absolom Aples & Sons. A mascot mannequin made of pillows is slouched on a beach chair beneath. An Australian flag bucket hat is stapled to the head and his button eyes are too small for his face, giving the impression of a shark.

They don't have it.

John Robert 'Bobby' Slake, 1929-2022, South Coast meatworks entrepreneur

The tens of thousands of frames of my film are spread across three computers, five USBs, two smart phones, an external drive and a floppy disk. My haphazard filing of these photographs makes even brief animated sequences impossible to finalise.

In one folder labelled March 2015 v6.1 FINAL draft, I find an out-of-focus close-up of Aloysha in prayer, a dingy vignette of the Karamazov Estate and an otherworldly snowscape which might be useable if not for the Nescafé tin in the background. Like Walt Disney, I'm committed to 30 frames a second. This unusable moment is therefore less than one hundred-thousandth of the film.

I try to plan the project out with storyboards, précis, spreadsheets, strategic analyses, Gan-charts, kanbans, and a sequence of somatic movements I dance, nude, in my bedroom. These processes reveal the same conclusion: at the rate I've been going for the last ten years, the film will take a lifetime to finish.

But even this is optimistic. I am going backwards. In the old days, I would tell Mum and my Monopoly friends I had hours of footage to edit. But now, as I scroll, shallow-breathed, through the labyrinth of files, I find less usable frames than there were before. I have also been gradually dismantling my sets. The Abbey is down to its foundations. Even the Sisyphean satisfaction of futile progress is denied me. I am losing ground.

I hire a Personal Achievement Coach to get me back on track. He is an accredited hypnotist—clinical and stage—and has a popular Instagram account full of clips of him deadlifting his wife. We have our first session kayaking down the Yarra, him pulling three strokes to each of my one.

'You need to actually say it.' The skyline shines in his wraparounds.

'I am not a fiduciary obituarist,' I say. 'I am a Dostoyevsky stop-motion animator who happens to work for a bank.'

'Yes!' he howls. 'YES YES YES!'

As we pass into the shadow of the Queen Street bridge, a gaunt rough sleeper stares.

Gabby in Bed

Finegan Kruckemeyer

2nd Prize

The first thing I notice is just how far from the ocean it is.

She could have gone anywhere. And who knows, she might have gone anywhere—I have no idea about her in-between years. But now, as her fire dies down, as her life runs out, she is here, in a tiny town, on a thankless street, in a forgotten flat which is part of a forgotten block of flats, so so far from the ocean.

I pull my car up out the front, step out, and immediately have that niggling whisper of a thought about whether or not I should leave it here. It's not a kind thought—it's one full of judgment and cruelty, and I banish it quickly, back into a corner of my brain I hope never needs unpacking.

The street is silent and the lawn out the front of the block exists in two states. Maybe one-third is mown but still unimpressive, clumsy lines of yellowing stubble. And then—at a point of exasperation—the mowing has stopped and left two-thirds shin-high and mangy, weeds and grass competing. At that moment of distinction, about halfway down a plodding row, the lawnmower lies right where it died. I know this because its housing has been removed and lies beside it, along with a rusted spanner. Who the mower was, what became of him, if he will ever return—I have no answers.

The front door to the units contains a very threatening sign about what will happen to trespassers, and also a completely broken door handle. It feels like a caretaker decided it was easier to print the sign than fix the latch. I risk it, and push my way inside. The 'Hello' I call out echoes in the ghostly stairwell. This building was grand once—but just sad now. I wade through its sadness and begin to climb—her note said 3A, so I aim for the third floor. I pass a box that explains: *in case of emergency, break glass.* And someone did break it. And whatever was inside—held by those two bent clips—is gone now. And I wonder what the emergency was.

On level three, the corridor is so still, the doors so identical, the air so patient that I feel like no one has ever walked here before. My shadow is the first shadow to rise up this wallpaper, my foot the first to tread upon this floorboard. The microbes in my exhaling breath are the first ever organisms in this ecosystem—a grand biological evolution will begin from this moment and span a billion years and end with gods and giants. I hear a wheezing cough, behind the thin wall to my left, and somehow recognise my mother's tired lungs. I could just turn and walk back the way I came. But I don't. I knock at her door.

I push with a flat, fearful palm and the wood swings on pained hinges. The room inside is both worse than I imagined, and also what I imagined.

'When I run out of dishes, I just buy more dishes.'

She stands in the bedroom doorway, leaning on the frame and laughing at my expression.

'Your life,' I mutter.

'And no one else's,' she says, and it sounds cruel. Cruel and sad.

Gabby moves slowly and painfully about the room, leaning on things every so often, with a sure sense of what will hold her and what would give way. Things that look rigid she avoids, while a tower of old newspapers supports her well. She opens the fridge and removes a plastic bottle of sparkling water, breaking the seal and pouring it out into two cups that sit pristine by the sink. They are the only two clean things in miles and I can see they have been waiting for this day.

She returns the bottle to the fridge, even though it holds so little water. Enough that she could have topped up our glasses. Too little for it to ever warrant a future drink, let alone a chilled one. For some reason that decision makes less sense to me than anything else encountered and I consider arguing, but she looks at me and I understand we are both skirting the edge of a large and dark forest, and step back.

'Thank you.'

She shrugs, takes her glass, walks to the bedroom. Collecting mine from the sink, I follow.

Gabby puts the glass on a bedside table that looks like an architect's model of a city, dystopian and precarious. She sits on the bed and then rotates on her thin bum, her back finding an impossible stack of pillows, legs laid out on the blanket. Her knees remain slightly bent and I know she cannot straighten them anymore. She doesn't offer me a seat, and there is no place she could, so I stand awkwardly in the doorway holding my water, but not drinking it.

'It's not poison.'

'I know it's not.'

But still I wait for her to drink first. She doesn't, and I feel the forest looming.

'Thanks for coming.'

'Thanks for telling me where to come.'

'But you'd have liked me to let you know a few years sooner.'

'Or not at all.'

It's mean, what I just said, but she smiles at it. I know she speaks this language of gentle violence well, that she has for years—muttering at teenagers in shops, chastising confused tourists—and when using it too, I see the first real spark of kinship in her eyes. Those eyes that are still so so alive, even if every other part of the structure is crumbling.

'How old are you now?'

'52.'

'And I haven't seen you since you were nine.'

'Correct.' It's a strange word to use, but I get my reasoning.

'You two didn't try to track me down,' says Gabby. 'Didn't come looking for me.'

I say nothing, just take a sip of my poisoned water.

'You didn't have to. I wasn't fishing. Just surprised me that you didn't.'

'We made something new. Emma came into our lives pretty soon after.'

'With the long plaits.' She notices my confusion. 'I saw her at the funeral.'

'Were you…? I didn't know you were there?'

'I know.'

'Where were you sitting?'

Gabby smiles. She likes the imbalance, information held by one and wanted by another. She swivels her finger in the air and smiles.

'Around.'

That answer makes me tired.

She reaches down then, under her bed, suddenly lurching her body downwards. Like she's reaching for a weapon. Which it's not. Or not

17

obviously one—I feel like anything could be weaponised, by either one of us, in this moment. She smiles at this and removes a book.

'Bang.'

Suddenly very serious, she opens the big chaotic volume out on her knees, paperwork spilling onto the floor, unchased.

'Come on then.'

I finish my water, place the empty glass on the floor (a mad decision but one that goes completely unnoticed) and walk over, standing beside her, high where she is low, her hair thin, her skull veins. She pores over the book.

'This explains it.'

'What?'

'It. Everything. You came here for explanations.'

'That's not true. I don't really know why I came here.'

'Alright, then—I know why for both of us. You have a gap. Your life has a gap. Me—I'm what wasn't there. So here. Fill in the gap.'

'You could just tell me.'

She scoffs. 'Fuck talking. I'm bitter and old. Everything I say sounds mean. It'll be tainted—you'll hear it as mean. You'll miss the information 'cause you'll be angry. Fair enough too.'

She slams it shut just as abruptly as she opened it and holds it up, staring up at me like our years and our roles are reversed. 'This is easier.'

I am lost for words. I take the book—it's both really heavy and really fragile. I hold it painfully, and delicately. The proximity feels funny now and I return to my doorway, half in and half out of this moment, a correct place to observe it from.

'If it's just about the...scrapbook. Or diary, or whatever this is. You could have just sent it to me. Sent me this instead of your address.'

She nods.

'Yeah.'

Nods again.

'Yeah, that's true. I don't have an answer for that.'

She lies back on the pillows—they wheeze as she leans her meagre weight on them, tired of her like the whole world is tired of her. I guess she's about to sleep, that the chat's over and now I go. But I can't.

'So that's it?'

'What is?'

'This. You tell me where you live. You let me in.'

'You let yourself in.'

'You give me a book. And you go to bed. No explanation.'

'The book is the explanation.'

'Your life is obviously ending, Gabriella.'

'*Gabriella.* Ha.'

'It's obvious you're dying. Dad just died, you're facing your own mortality, so you reach out to me. But then.'

'What?'

'You get scared.'

'I'm not scared.

'You're terrified. Terrified and hiding in bed.'

She roars and it is like an animal.

'I've been more places in this bed than you'll ever know!'

It is the strangest sentence, delivered with the strangest anger, answering nothing at all, but at the same time more finite than anything she might have ever said. She collapses back, the pillows sighing.

'Just read the book.'

And my mother gives up on me and simply lies, staring up at the sky. I follow her gaze—a pack of matches is held in place, taped to the ceiling. It makes no sense. None of it does.

I am left—like I was left the first time, but the mirror image of it. Her departure is one of stillness now, and it forces me to go.

I walk numbly out of the doorway and through the rubbish of a life. For a moment, I consider flicking a lighter and simply erasing everything. Letting a fire climb from outcrop to outcrop, across surfaces, over newspapers, fridges melting, glasses exploding, the whole building eating itself. I don't do this—but maybe just because I'm not sure I would make it out in time? The answer to that sits in a corner of my brain unvisited.

I shut the door behind me. I carry the book. I descend the stairs. I pass the broken box. There was never an emergency. There was just fear disguised as toughness. Just Gabby grasping desperately at tools. But not knowing where to aim. Who to call. What to say. Simply ending up alone, in a bed, cradling a fire extinguisher, smelling smoke in every place imaginable.

The Sins of Coal Ridge

A.J. Henry

3rd Prize

Bloated wombats littered the roadside along the Razor Back. Hot pink Xs were sprayed across the animal's backs. The carcasses awaited an inglorious send-off in the rear-loader on its way down to Pitch Town. Every day new bodies appear.

Come daybreak, Morrie Cavendish travelled the Razor Back to the mail distribution depot to sort his beat before returning to the ridge. Morrie left the window down, even in winter, to puff from a pipe as big as a sheep's horn. On seeing short, muscular legs pointing skyward, he laughed.

'Gone to God.'

Morrie fancied they'd do the same to him when he went. With road-kill lingering in his tar-scorched nostrils, he urged his van, with its blood and fur-smeared bull bar, upwards.

The head frame stood at the back of Coal Ridge. It towered over the district on spidery legs. Winding drums whispered when wind brushed the cables. The miners who rode the vertical hoist into the pit called it the gallows frame. When men worked a seam in one of the districts, they rostered a gasman. Rupert Wheams routinely inspected the alarm on his semi-conductor sensors and electro-chemical diffusion barriers for gases. After a dry bearing on a conveyor's idler ignited coal dust, the main-gate filled with toxic afterdamp.

Two men died.

Rumours lingered—why had the gasman not reported for duty that day?

Coal trucks no longer barrelled down the Razor Back to Port Kembla. Old miners passed on, or were tucked up in nursing homes on the coast with their secrets and black lung. The pithead was now abandoned. The headframe surrendered to rust.

The chamber of business erected a commemorative arch over the road.

21

Franz, the Workers Club secretary, unveiled the plaque.

'Youz all know coal made this town. Before coal there was nuttin', just bush and wombats. Coal made this town into the proud and prosperous place it is. It's only fittin' we remember the blokes who toiled to build it. Coal gave us everyfing,' Franz said, thrusting his fist.

No one raised a toast or muttered here-here, or God rest. Tommo scratched his balls. Maureen shifted to one side. Mandy gave Kali a sidelong glance. Only Madge Wilson surveyed the arch.

Early on the day Morrie Cavendish died, he wove a scarlet ribbon through wire fencing off the pit. This ribbon sat beside a somewhat faded one, and the one beside it was in tatters. Other cloth had since weathered to thread. He peered through twists of wire as he did when he last saw her: Pretty Avril Wheams with pearly skin and hair to quieten Flame Trees.

At midday Friday, knock-off time, Morrie downed shots with Yong, Gaz, and Tommo in the Workers Club. He argued with Kali, claiming she short-changed him, and called Franz a no-hoper.

'Me third wife was the best. Can't wait to see her again,' he said, cigarette ash sprinkling the tabletop. Everyone knew his third wife was a smoker. Although they amputated her legs, she puffed on with a two-fingered salute to the universe.

'Was she the love of your life?' Mandy said.

Morrie didn't answer, but simply gazed at swirling smoke from his cigarette.

When Morrie hanged himself from the commemorative arch, it unhinged the town. Tommo saw the fire crew from the Workers Club car park and raced down the ridge to stop the school bus. When Todd found out, he was shitty. He wanted to see a real dead person, and not dead ones in his head. Kali told him it was not like a normal dead person and he should feel sad, even though Jessica told Madge Williams that Morrie would burn for his sins.

Mandy and Jessica held up poly tarps while first responders took Morrie down.

Madge Williams directed the whole thing like a band master looking for a lost manuscript. Mandy whispered to Jessica that she was a meddling old cow, anyway.

The ambos said the phenomenon was not unusual in cases like this. The noose put pressure on the cerebellum, creating the occurrence.

That night, the town gathered. Mandy said she will never wipe the image from her memory and Kali and Jessica agreed. Morrie dangling with a terminal erection was like, hello, forever. Tommo said Todd was a sicko for wanting to see a dead person. Jessica turned on him, demanding he apologise.

'Kid's normal,' Jessica said. 'Curious 'tis all.'

Kali said it was okay as Tommo should leave the bar because he's had a skinful.

Franz didn't like her attitude towards a regular customer. He irked Kali and, deep down, she thought her boss was a creep.

Gaz reckoned they should rename the town Angel Lust in memory of Morrie. Yong agreed. But only because he thought the old guy down the street would move out.

East Buringee, No. 2, was a deep pit. A bord mine with tunnels crisscrossing. When the surrounding layers shifted, it reverberated through its subterranean corridors. Pitmen called it the bump, a sound to unnerve young and old alike. Sometimes, in the still hours when the pit moved, townsfolk said it was the ghost of Avril Wheams.

Authorities never found her body. Forensics could not carry out an investigation because the pit was unstable.

The mining museum formed part of the Workers Club. Volunteers ran it, but no one bothered. The school has fewer students each year, not like the days before. Now, kids go to schools in Pitch Town. Yong's shop and the Workers Club are the only businesses to survive.

Kali pulled beers at the club. She preloaded a few before starting her shift because she said it got her through the night. One time, when driving to work, she crashed into the vacant block where townsfolk bury pets.

Franz wanted to fire Kali after the accident, but the town turned on him. Gaz, Kali's husband, towed the Hyundai away before the police found out. Franz was a perv, anyway. Morrie swore he saw Franz pull down a backpacker's top in the carpark. Franz denied it and threatened to sue him.

Franz controlled the Workers Club to his rules when it came to intoxication.

'If they push money across the bar, keep it comin'. Besides, the town's so far from a cop shop, no one gives a shit.'

It was true. The police rarely came this far along the ridge unless it was serious.

Good Shoes

Andrea Rowe

Highly Commended

She wears her sweat and piss like a coat. Wrapped warm in a stench that curls its way up unsuspecting nostrils, she is propelled, uninterrupted, towards the counter. Shadows sidestep behind shelves. She can see them— she isn't immune to their twitching and tutting. They're sniffing her air and quick marching away, beyond her odour.

Tarli rolls a wave of phlegm loudly, an 'Up Yours' mucus curl to the room. The bloke ahead of her rapidly leaves the queue. Works a treat, every time. Fiona's on today. She's all right. The sort that looks you in the eye and gives you the once over. Scanning for the bruising trouble that falls your way, and not the trouble you'll bring. She isn't like the others staring at their screens with over-eager focus.

Tarli fumbles in pockets, and slaps the library card on the counter. 'G'day Fi, can I've an hour thanks?'

Fiona gives her one of those smiles that show sad and happy all at once. It reminds her of that cloth doll Gran made her when she was six. Yellow woollen hair and sewn on face—happy one side, then flip it 'round and there's a curve of closed eyes and a stitched tear drop. A bit like Gran's face as she handed over her keys to the caravan, giving her a chance to stay put for winter and try quitting. Gran all happy-sad, patting her arm and passing her a box of canned food. Tarli wanted to make a go of it, but she stuffed that up too. Scored a hit for old time's sake, fell asleep in her puke and woke to Gran standing in the annexe, tipped all the way over into sadness.

Fiona nods. 'Pod 24 OK with you today?' They both know what that means. There's an after-school group in, mums who hover and smart mouth kids. Number 24 is a corner pod with an egg chair to herself—just for the hour. Be great if she could book it for a whole night—she'd curl up in those purple arms, the smell of safety.

'Yeah, thanks.'

Tarli shoves her backpack under her feet, pulls her hoodie back and logs her password in—Gran's name. The screen's reflection outlines her nest of hair, looped all crazy from the winds. She pulls herself back from the screen as her Facebook profile appears.

There she is, hugging her ripped knees, fingers gripping the tops of Doc Martens. Cam's old leather belt twisted around her arm from wrist to elbow, hiding bruises. Eyes smudged with black eyeliner and defiance. Or fear. She forgets which.

Those Docs held up good, plum purple with thick-ass soles. When the laces snapped, she flogged replacements off sneakers under the jetty. Some poor runner went in for a swim and came out to a laceless jog home. She felt bad about it, but those Docs, they were good shoes. They took her places. She almost had to leave them behind once. Never should've let Cam talk her into crashing that holiday house for a hit, kip, and dip. Course there'd be security cruising by as they fired up the spa. Two burly blokes strolling around the corner as they scrambled for the wall, pulling backpacks and boots with them. Bloody Cam—it was a close call. Just like Cam was. Gran always said he'd bring her to her knees.

Tarli scrolls down the screen, peering into her old life.

All those faces. Cousins, aunts and uncles smiling and taking the piss in those lounge rooms and backyards. The grins you give when you've slept in a soft bed, turned dials to keep you fed, showered, warm, shut in, shut out.

Smiling faces she used to know. People who knew the old her.

'Tarli Dingaling,' That's what Gran called her.

'Tarli Dingaling choked on a chicken wing,' The smaller of the cousins would chant.

'Tarli Dingaling's got a goober nose ring.'

We all had a name, and the rhymes came easy. The cousins never let you down there.

That mad pack of cousins that came together every summer, bags heaving with towels and cricket bats, boogie boards and Nintendos. The annexe smelling of farts, wet sand, and heaving with noise.

'You bugger's give me some peace,' Gran would yell. 'Get down to the beach.' She and Mum would shuffle the deck, stretching their legs under the card table. The clatter of cousins would tear off, yanking towels and packets of Twisties, tripping over guy ropes and scattering through the scrub to the Foreshore.

She's right back there now—that year of Christmas money and stockpiling her vouchers to sing those purple Docs towards her. Those kicks were all she'd think of. It was Paul who gave her a wink with an extra $20 to get her across the line. Mum, Gran and Aunty Jussy would open their Bundy and Cokes as Paul stretched his spaghetti arms out.

'Ka-Ching! Tarli Dingaling don't know a thing.'

Yeah so, she was a bit dumb at the schoolbooks and slower at counting. She never got those science and maths tricks tumbling over themselves, or spy movie plots at the Drive In. Yeah, Tarli Dingaling don't know a thing, all right. But it was all a laugh. She gave back just as good. That's the way of family—give back, take it. Give back, take it. Till Paul took it too far. A wallop on the back. Flick to her head. Kick up the arse. An elbow jam into a wall was his speciality.

'Whoops, clumsy bugger, watch yourself.' He'd dig his stubby fingers into her arms as he righted her, hot breath hissing 'Frigging cow,' into her ear.

Tarli Dingaling just can't win.

The truth buried itself in the stories they all wanted to hear, not the ones she whispered to the others when Paul was down at the TAB.

Tarli Dingaling's having a whinge.

Mum never believed her, no chance of that. And Gran thought he was the moonbeam of son-in-laws. Fixed her place up. Mowed the lawns. Took her to the RSL. He was Mum's saviour too, for a while.

Tarli Dingaling's copping a beating. Tarli Dingaling's nicking the money tin.

By the time she walked her sorry Doc Martin soles into Cam's life, Paul seemed like a frigging picnic.

Tarli Dingaling's in full swing. Tarli Dingaling's shooting a syringe.

Back on screen, her messages glow red with questions from the cousins. 'Tarli, Tarli—what'd you do to yourself girl?' 'Where are you Tarli? What the fuck is going on?' 'Don't you dare come 'round here again. Do you know what you've done to the family?' The curser blinks accusingly.

Their faces, scrubbed clean of mistakes, stare through the screen. She rubs at the start of a headache.

Looks like Paul's moved on and Mum's got a new fella. All for nothing then. And the first grandchild from Darren and Lexie has Gran smiling. Cute kid, and a brand-new name for Gran to find a rhyme for. That's the way of family, coming and going, making room for the new ones, closing the door on the ones who bring the trouble. That'll do for today—just a check in to see what they're up to.

Tarli clicks off the screen. Fiona gives her a wave as she pulls on her backpack, re-ties a shoelace and heads towards the door, keen to get ahead of the school kids. Her milk crate is stuffed out of sight behind the library skip. Hauling it out, she spots Razzy crab-stepping up the road, that sideways sway he gets when he's had a hit of the whiz. He's all lit like George Street, flapping the air with his good hand and shouting Yugoslav words all jagged and jumbled.

Razzy gives her a nod and veers off towards the life-saving club. He'll be good for a hit tonight. She could do with that. The air feels punchy, and there's a big bruise of clouds all hunched over across the bay. What's that bluesy song Aunt Jussy used to sing when she had a skinful? 'There's a storm coming, slouching down the road.' The song was belting out from the annexe when Paul brought her back from the Plaza, her gripping those new Docs two sizes too big, temple aching from that unexpected fist as they walked from the carpark. He'd give and take hard that bastard.

Probably worth setting up near the club herself tonight. The back gate's missing a padlock, so it's easy enough to haul her gear through, but there's no sign of Razzy. Maybe he can give her a leg up to crawl through the window for the showers later—been a while since the last one.

Tarli pulls off her Docs, double wraps them in a shopping bag and nudges them into the crate between her towel and her tuna cans. Pulling off her socks, she peels a band-aid from her heel, and examines the blister. That's going to sting tomorrow. But she'll shove those shoes back anyway.

The afternoon's coming in cold. She slides into her sleeping bag all sticky-wet from salt mist, careful not to let the broken welt catch on the fabric. She'd like to dream of the old caravan tonight. Flicking towels at the cousins. Mum shaking sand from her book. The slick of salt drying on skin as they head for showers. Tarli remembers wiping the sand off her Docs with her damp towel before heading to the carnival. Her purple feet swinging from the Pirate Ship. Gran and Mum hollering below. She soared up there in that cloud-sky.

A good dream in good shoes.

Tarli smells them before she sees them. Then she hears them. The waft of fish and chips plays with her stomach. There's still a few more hours till she can grab a feed from the van down by the hall, but these chips—they smell good. Her head's out of the sleeping bag before she has time to think straight.

The stocky ones jumps back, 'Bloody hell, what are you looking at?' A lean face peers at her through a sideways fringe, flicking chips at his mates. She's taken them by surprise, five hooting teens full of bravado and boredom. She's got their interest now. She wishes she didn't.

'Ha! You crapped your pants Leachy.'

'Shut it—saw you lot pack ya dacks,' yaps the Chip Flicker.

'Yeah? So, what're you looking at?' He steps towards Tarli, then rears back. She watches his deep swallow of dry retch.

'Gwhaar, that's rank!'

She turtles her head back into her sleeping bag. Right now, her smell is her only weapon, but she takes cover for what's to come, quietly pulling at the zipper, sweaty fists curled.

Tarli Dingaling's ready to swing.

'Carn Leachy, leave her mate.'

She remembers back to the cousins, the pack of them pulling at each-other's arms when they saw Paul staggering towards them. Where's Razzy when she bloody needs him?

A wad of greasy paper hits her sleeping bag, and from inside she can hear the hiss of salt raining down.

'Bitch!'

Shoes shuffle. Feet scrape. The gate rattles. Their ribbing and hollering fades into the distance. She stays inside, cocooned, until even she can't hack the smell of herself. When Tarli pulls down the zipper and peers out, the crate is gone. She wrenches herself from the twist of bag and lunges towards the footpath. Down past the breakwater there's a swell of movement. They're playing some sort of game. Sideways swaggering, tossing and throwing something between themselves as they chart their way towards the jetty. Tarli slows to watch them, her bare toes pushing into the warm sand. Filtered.

A box arcs across the sunset—tubs, towel and Docs fly from the crate and disappear into the silky water. Good shoes submerged. Tarli feels herself launch with them. Washed clean. Released.

The Bendigo Marxist Ladies' Auxiliary
Amanda Hildebrandt

Commended

The Rembrandt was not a Rembrandt, that much had been established. It was the first item on the agenda, and had been resolved within five minutes. The third item was the state of the kitchen, but that was tabled by Ben, who wasn't up for a domestic discussion so soon after bickering with his wife over toast crumbs in the butter. The second item on the agenda was the new-captions project, which, to everyone's relief, Silvia volunteered to manage.

Silvia had harboured doubts about Ben's subscription to the cult of Agile, with its sprints and scrums and standing meetings, but this morning's outcome had been swift and provocative, putting Silvia in high spirits and back at her desk before ten. It would have been earlier, but she'd been detained by Ellis, who was moping about the Rembrandt judgement.

He'd been the one to find the painting, under a forgotten censer and some moderately interesting gold plate, in a Bendigo manse which now belonged to Silvia's old housemate. The solid perfume in the censer had melted, stamping a skewed, greasy halo on the left cheek of Saint Cecelia.

Silvia understood his mistake, his excitement at the *impasto* brushwork and the depiction of the saint as a lay person, but her meticulous, annotated report disputed his attribution, and he was making her pay with clumsy intimations of betrayal, here, in the kitchen, with its crusted microwave and sticky benches and motley collection of chipped teacups promoting bygone auction houses. Silvia offered to make amends by returning the debunked painting to the manse—Ellis would have been indiscreet about the value of what he thought he'd found, and would now be reluctant to face the owner. Ellis accepted the gesture, as they all always did—Silvia had earned a reputation for tying up loose ends, taking on the jobs no one else wanted.

Today, her forbearance granted her temporary custody of the painting, so that she could quietly confirm what she suspected: that the Rembrandt was not only not a Rembrandt, but was not a painting of Saint Cecelia, and that the owner had known it all along.

Saint Cecelia, after Rembrandt, c.1684-1690, oil on canvas. Little is known about this painting, although the masterful treatment of light and skin tone suggests it may be a copy of a lost work from the Dutch Golden Age. The viol resting against the folds of the sitter's dress identifies her as Saint Cecelia, patron saint of music.

Courtesy of The Bendigo Marxist Ladies' Auxiliary.

It was seventeen years since Silvia had been to Bendigo. There was an air of *déjà vu*—of curious, dream logic—as she overlaid the map of her childhood with the material landscape before her. Large, glass-fronted palaces of global commerce rose from bulldozed blocks, adding a touch of anywhere-ness to the skyline, while the caramel, Gold-Rush-era buildings of Pall Mall looked on, filmy and still, as if they had drifted downstream two centuries ago, along with the alluvial gold. The bakeries were called *Boulangerie* and *Pasticceria*. Queues formed outside hole-in-the-wall coffee spots. Chancery Lane was colourful and close, while craft beer and tapas were verging on ubiquitous. Weekend trippers from Melbourne populated the craft and farmer's markets, staving off the Sunday evening *ennui* with local stone-baked bread and white mould cheese. Silvia was caught off guard by the industry, the *hum* of the place. It gave her the feeling that she hadn't paid attention when this had been her home, and it stood at odds with self-perception.

Some things hadn't changed. Silvia knelt in the garden of the old manse, helping Hannah weed around the seaside daisies, flowering white against the earthy orange of the terracotta bowl by the back door. The garden was wild, in need of secateurs and dead-heading. Hannah's grandmother had left the place to her, and she was sprucing it up for a quick sale, but for now the women worked slowly, catching up over the daisies. The returned artwork sat inside, on the kitchen table, between two mugs of tepid coffee. Despite the years between visits, they knew where they stood with each other, Silvia and Hannah. Hannah had always harboured a protestant suspicion of anything that looked like an icon, and Silvia—Silvia was an iconoclast, in the broadest sense. They had followed each other's careers, cheering from the side-lines. When Ellis had found the picture, filed in a crate of religious paraphernalia inside a boiler room cupboard, jammed shut with generations of paint and wallpaper, Hannah knew that she could rely on Silvia to get involved, to rationalise and de-sanctify.

As poor, Melbourne-bound art history students, Silvia and Hannah had once shared a room in a ramshackle Brunswick bungalow, making ginger beer in the carport laundry to sell on market days. They'd co-designed the label: thick, stylised rays of sunshine strobing around a tall, angular scaffold, silhouetted against the sunshine aura. The structure was instantly recognisable to a Bendigo local. Poppet heads like it had dotted the area during the Gold Rush-era, carrying miners and tools into the earth and back again. The poppet heads had gone now, except for those that had been polished and repurposed as tourist attractions—the architecture of the working class, now a symbol of leisure, distilled and consumed as a lesson in history.

Everything becomes something else. This was what Ben and Ellis and the others at the gallery couldn't reconcile, with their klaxon-calls about NFTs and the destruction of creativity. Silvia would have agreed, if she hadn't known that it wasn't the money they objected to, or the cost to the earth, or the baffling paradox that NFTs seemed to make less sense the more stand-up meetings they devoted to unpicking them. What offended Silvia's colleagues was the fact that the definition of art—after all this time –overthrew attempts at taxonomy, kept shifting, refusing to be constrained by logic and profit and all those things that look good on a spreadsheet.

Silvia and Hannah had appreciated this even in their undergraduate days, in the backyard of the Brunswick terrace, with their derivative ginger beer labels and their passing knowledge of Marxist art theory. They'd drag a tarpaulin over the bottles fermenting in the carport and sit on the back stairs, debating definitions with the earnest clumsiness of first-year art history majors, drinking the fruit of their labour, discussing the systemic pressures against women in art, plotting revolution as the beer fermented and the odd bottle exploded, staining the pavers with streams of yeasty, ginger-perfumed fizz. Only when the neighbours turned on their porch lights to investigate would they go inside, leaving their debate with the empty bottles on the back step.

They were inside now, in the kitchen of the old manse, washing the soil from their hands and reheating their coffees in the microwave—older, more cynical, but also more subtle. They had read more, absorbed more, and could spot the difference between perceived value and genuine novelty.

The painting, wrapped on the table between them, had been diminished, cheapened by the loss of title. It was no longer the recovered work of an old master. But if it could unfold and speak its history, it would show itself to be something rarer still: the signature of a woman, working in anonymity, in the small space permitted her, determined to create herself, to declare—for all those who doubted and dismissed her—that she was no copyist. She had been patient through the centuries, waiting for her audience, but for all the detective work in their profession, neither Hannah nor Silvia where to start looking for it.

Portrait of a woman, after Rembrandt, c.1684-1690, oil on canvas. The sitter, once thought to be Saint Cecelia, is now believed to be the wife of a wealthy, seventeenth-century merchant. The voluminous folds of gold velvet worn by the sitter indicate that her husband dealt in fine cloth, while the viol may be intended to represent her feminine accomplishments.

Courtesy of The Bendigo Marxist Ladies' Auxiliary.

Friday morning stand-ups were usually given over to weekly reviews and reminders that any food in the communal fridge would be cleared out by close of business. This morning, though, Silvia was moved to interrupt the flow of Ben's bullet-point agenda. The painting, now as good as authorless, had fallen from the schedule, and Silvia was surprised at the vehemence of her objection. Something about her reunion with Hannah—the chat about the old days, when they sprouted and lived small-batch ideals and the question was *is it art*, not *can we make a copy and call it an original*. Something that had value with one signature had become worthless with that signature removed. It was as if they claimed a mystical power: by the mere act of naming a thing, they brought that thing into existence. But the anonymity of the hand was the point of this work, and far more interesting than any lost old master. How many other works were out there, masquerading as *after* or *school of*, executed by women trying to find a space for expression? How many had slipped through the cracks, been misattributed, footnoted as the helpmates of the singular male genius they—Silvia included—had been primed to believe sprang, fully formed, into existence, from the thigh of Zeus, belittling the people—the *women*—that gave them recognition at the expense of their own?

Silvia said all this in the meeting, ignoring Ben's awkward attempts to regain control. When she finished, Ben tabled the discussion and moved to the third item on the agenda: progress on the new-captions project, to reflect the new direction of the gallery.

Silvia stood in the kitchen, which smelled faintly of boiled asparagus, waiting for her tea to steep. Ellis moved behind her to fetch a coffee cup. Silvia expected a lecture on the rewards of compromise or, at the very least, an I-told-you-so. Instead, Ellis told her that sometimes he felt like he was looking at an under-painting of himself, something familiar but obscured by layers of correction. Silvia tore the lid from her single-serve milk and stirred it into her mug. She watched the streaks of white fan out, distorting the dark tannin surface before they vanished, absorbed into an altered whole. It was lived experience, not training, that told her the painting they had uncovered in the old manse was a self-portrait of a pregnant woman. Underneath the grease spot left by the censer perfume, Silvia recognised those same pin-sized pricks of pigmentation on the sitter's face as she had seen when she was ten, and her mother was pregnant with her little sister.

But lived experience had little worth in the world of desk research and definitive attributions. Silvia suddenly realised how unjust—how *unwise*— that was. She and Hannah had been on the right track, all those years ago. She would find the way back to those days, when they held the subversive in plain sight, and celebrated the communal, and saw through the over-painting, through to the labour sunk into its creation, to all the hands that had called it into existence. And if she needed a name—a caption—for the movement, that would be as simple as turning to the label on a bottle of ginger beer.

Self-portrait of a woman, unknown artist, c.1684-1690. The pigmentation on the face of the sitter suggests that the artist was pregnant at the time of painting. The relaxed folds of gold velvet indicate that she was in her second trimester. No documentary evidence has been found to identify the artist. Seventeenth-century women had few freedoms—after giving birth, the artist may never have had the opportunity to paint again. Had she done so, we may speak of her as meeting and surpassing the talent and renown of her male contemporaries, without the benefit of their formal training.

Courtesy of The Bendigo Marxist Ladies' Auxiliary.

After

Darcy-Lee Tindale

Commended

On the first night,
I told you I loved you. When I squeezed it in code into the centre of your palm. But you were distracted by the air that smelt of burnt eucalytus. The evening sky was a haze of smoky grey, blown in from the Blue Mountains, aglow in red. Our eyes settled on the city's skyline before we said goodnight. Then you bowed your head and offered me your ruddy lips to peck, and in the palm of your hand, I tap-tap-tapped. Three seconds. I-love-you. Tap-tap-tap. Only, you missed it.

On the second night,
with adoring hands, I told you, *I loved you.* When my nails etched it in brail across the ridge of your back. But you were distracted by the crack in the ceiling, and only laughed when I told you it had just appeared—from the sudden temperature and moisture fluctuation in my bedroom. Then I saw how deep your dimples could dig into your cheeks. We spent the night caught up in twisted bedsheets and damp limbs. And after—after— in the wee small hours, naked and exposed, you whispered all your hidden things.

One night,
we strolled idly home with our elbows linked. We had been lavish with our drinks.
'Lavish is a nicer word than pissed,' you said.
'We got a little lavished!' I snorted, tipping back my head.
My mouth was scented with garlic. Italian music had become an earworm for the rest of the evening. It was the first time I had tried black pasta and learnt how to pronounce Pinot Grigio correctly.
'Not to be confused with its French cousin, Pee noh gree,' you said.
As we strolled down the uneven path, my grip on your elbow tightened. With our courtship now locked in, I felt your body smile.

One afternoon,
with my toothbrush packed, I turned my back on my crumbling apartment with the crack in the ceiling. I closed the door on my past and bounced down the rotting timber steps that made you say, 'Careful, one day you'll fall,' every time you climbed them.

I crossed over the Bridge, landing on your side.

I stood raw in front of your house and watched you through the window's blue hue, framed by decorative corners in burnt orange and green.

You opened the door, scooped me up in a promise, and the house and I tried to get acquainted.

But—but I heard the house say, 'Three weeks, tops.'

So, I rubbed my scent all over it. Marked my territory. Infused new smells.

Three weeks later, I was still there.

One morning,
I saw flaws. Minor. Nothing I couldn't fix. The wet towel on the bathroom floor which you stepped over. The coffee cup that sat on the dresser for days—days. Its contents first turned milky white and then olive green. And while I watched the subtle changes, it was invisible to you.

But after—after—just like the bubbling green mould that floated on the surface of the forgotten coffee cup, I brewed with the need for a few drastic changes.

One night,
I met your friends. The pub was dark and loud. The cement floor echoed the chink of schooners dumped on tables.

I was nervous. A headache already. Turning unspoken dialogues over and over and over and over and over in my head. My brain was still cartwheeling when I met them. I wasn't ready.

I laughed at their jokes. Tried to flirt a little. Your friends were hard work.

Amongst the frowning fields of brows, I tried to win them over.

My old days of bourbon and coke were now behind me. I tried to swallow liquid gold infused in bubbles. You noticed the delicate flecks of glitter in my eyeshadow and liked my eyelash extensions, but you failed to notice my glossed nails that scratched an SOS into your knee.

Scratch-scratch-scratch. Three seconds. I-knee'd-you. Scratch-scratch-scratch. Only, you ignored it.

Your friends had sensed my friendlessness. Asked, 'Where were they? My friends?' And, 'Why had it taken me so long to meet them? His friends?'

I skipped away from the questions, weaving between bar stools and drunken chatter as I made my way to the ladies. I could feel their eyes throwing spears into my back. But it was their protest, their claim that I should not dwell in your home, their claim that I held a lawless passport to pass through the hallway of your home that spurred me on to dismantle them.

After—after I said, 'Your friends are dicks.'

I convinced you of that.

Later, together in bed, I sealed the conviction with open legs. My ankles locked together in the dip of your back.

One dark night,
with our cheeks pressed warmly together, I pointed up towards the constellations.

'Look, the saucepan,' I said.

'Orion,' you corrected.

This is where I stopped. I simmered. Boiling scorpions in a pot—in a saucepan.

Unaware, you pointed to Sirius. Your stars were richer in the sky.

Late one evening,
we stumbled across the heat of our neighbour's argument. Their front door was open wide for all to hear. We were stung from their words. We sensed the end of the relationship before the fight was finished. We hurried inside and looked at each other, wide-eyed and mouths gaping.

'We will never be like that,' you said.

'Never,' I said.

But we forgot to close the front door to our own home.

After a few months,

the laundry and I became estranged. The lounge room and I became inseparable. I preferred 'in' to 'out'. I preferred 'seasons' to 'movies'. I preferred you put on something clean, rather than ask me if I'd washed something you fancied to wear.

The house glared at me. It held me up in the hallway. Like a customs checkout. I was a foreigner in your life.

'Passport please? Visa? Visiting or business? Length of stay? LENGTH OF STAY?' I heard the hall monitor ask.

Not wanting to be blocked at the border, I stamped my rite of passage with the heel of my *Jimmy Choo* pumps into the wall. Your friends inspired me to do that—stamp my passport.

I moved the bookshelf to hide my hallmark. You didn't even notice.

Midnight,

my keys and patience lost. I stood on the lawn dripping from rain and yelled. But the house would not open up to me. I kicked through the silence of the night—and the front door— breaking a fresh passage.

This is the moment, I knew, the house went dead inside.

'Who does that?' You asked. 'Who kicks in a door?'

'Me,' I replied.

It took eight days and eight hundred dollars before I fixed it. With my fingers crossed, I hoped the new door was a fresh start. But replacing the new doesn't make the old go away.

You used that moment to mock and joke. You stung me with sarcastic jibs to make me laugh, but also to remind and punish me for what I did on that wet midnight.

One afternoon,

our points of view collide. The car engine idled, almost stalled at the red light. We fumed at each other, emitting hatred, which filtered out through the crack in the window.

A woman in a car beside us discretely wound up her window so we could cough pollution into each other's faces without her listening. I knew she was praying for the lights to turn green.

I slapped both palms against the passenger window, rammed my face into the glass and screamed at her, 'What the fuck are you looking at?'

The heat of my words fogged the window.

You dropped your head in disgust and asked, 'Are you out of your fucking mind?'

It took all of seventeen seconds to get to this moment, and after—after—seven thousand seconds to get out of it.

The next morning,
I opened a window to clear the air.

One night,
panicked and running late, you laid blame.

'Where the fuck did you put it? Stop moving shit. Leave shit alone.'

I said, 'I never moved your shit.'

'Stop fucking with me,' you said.

'Okay,' I said, 'I'll stop fucking you.'

One night—and the next, then the next,
work held you back. You toiled. Then you came home and washed away the grub.

I sat on the bathroom floor and watched you shower. My arse pressed against the mosaic tiles, while my mind pressed against assembled images. I tried to see a larger picture, but I was missing a few small pieces.

I looked at where my lips had kissed, my tongue had traced, wondering about other mouths that had sucked—explored—and tasted your skin. New mouths—perhaps?

My image of you a fog, as you filled the room with steam.

You scrubbed away clues. Brushed the lies from your mouth with mint. Washed away the muck. Now clean of any dirt.

But—but my tongue dug for details. I filled in the blanks. Only, I said too much, too much, too much, too—too much, until I could no longer stuff the words back in my mouth.

'Your mouth is filth,' you said, tossing the cake of soap at my head.

I picked it up from the floor. Licked the soap's sudsy icing. Sucked the cake with the same erotic smile as when I licked and sucked on you. Then. I took a large bite. And chewed, and chewed, and chewed.

You stared.

The water in the taps ran cold.

Our last month,
you doubted our future.

I begged, 'I'll lick the front pavement to prove I love you.'

On our street. *Our* street. On my hands and knees, in down dog pose, I licked the footpath.

'You're out of your fucking mind,' you said—again—and again.

Every time we kissed after—after—you tasted of asphalt.

The flavour of your mouth and body was irreversible.

Our last week,
I slipped between each crack.

I weaved between lover and tormentor.

You urged for solitude. I begged for gratitude.

We threw things. Smashed things. Okay, I smashed things, expensive things. You threatened to change the locks. You begged for space.

I pointed up to the sky and said, 'There, have all the space you want. Go visit fucking Onion!'

'Orion,' you corrected.

I threw a saucepan. Then spent the rest of the night holding ice against your forehead. I kept saying, 'Please, please, please, please don't tell anyone what happened.'

But I never apologised.

Our last day,
you sent a text.

'Coward,' I replied. Followed by an angry face emoji.

That morning, we cut ties.

So, I swung an axe.

I cut through the bullshit and nostalgia, chopping away at the air and spent time. Wasting each stroke. Outraged at my little moments of idée fixe. Finally, free at last from my fixation, you were out of my head.

My aim? The centre of the bed. I sliced through the memories of our sweat and sex and left a notch on the post of your bed. Your bed.

Then, sapped and worn, I ran a bath. Naked, I lay still and soaked in your words. Clear now. Warm and pink skinned. My nipples broke through the water's surface and were the colour of lavender: purple and blue hue.

Rosy-cheeked, I gouged out my pain, carving out great chunks of grief with the tip of the axe. I filled the bath with my raging red anger. Then, before I left, I heard the water pipes—tap. Tap-tap-tap. Three seconds. Tap-tap-tap.

'Good-bye-you,' said the house.

Only, you weren't there to hear it, after—after our last day.

The Waves

Glenn Stuart Beatty

Local Award

The waves are crashing on the cliffs and there are seabirds circling in the wind under a grey sky. The man does not know the names of these birds but thinks that they might be gulls of some description and he sings to himself a line from an old song locked in his memory about seabirds and screaming gulls and despair. The cries of the birds rise and fall on the wind that has blown all the way, unimpeded, from Antarctica to batter against these rocks. The icy water stings the man's face as he walks, along the edge of the cliff, as he does every day, looking out to sea, remembering and dreaming.

In the distance, he thinks he hears the sound of a dog barking. He has not met his neighbour but has seen and heard him from afar work his sheep. When he rented his house from the old couple in town, he was told that it was a close-knit community but also one that respected people who wanted to be alone. The stone cottage was at the end of the road. It rained a lot and the ground was boggy with patches of peat that he hadn't expected to find, thinking of peat as something from the northern hemisphere. The smell of the peat wasn't unpleasant when he burned the dried bricks he had found left in his woodshed next to the house.

The man remembered that he hadn't eaten all day and it was already well into the afternoon and would soon be cold and dark.

He remembered what Durrell had written about another island in a book he had read when he was young, in another house, in another place, and thought, at the time, that it was a good book. Durrell's island was in the Mediterranean, where he said that to go there to heal, to rebuild, a man must be truly sick. It may have been a sickness that brought the man here in the first place, but he no longer had a name for that sickness, and he didn't much care.

There was nowhere else to go, and he had come to the bottom of this island at the bottom of the country, wind-blown, a place of secrets.

It had been a gradual journey over thirty years, this odyssey of his.

This past was now waiting for him in the black stone cottage not unlike the crofter's houses he had seen in the highlands and islands of Scotland back in another life. Now this past had drifted down from the mainland for some form of reckoning, some calling to accounts that he would have to face. He was bemused that it had found him here given he had covered his tracks so well over the years, making himself invisible, a ghost on a headland, wrapped in mist, but not, it seems, invisible to other ghosts from other lives and other days. He thought for a moment that it would be simpler to walk off the edge of the cliff, a moment of pain, of horror and regret perhaps, and then to be covered by the black water. He shook his head at the thought that it would be too easy that way and turned back towards the cottage, back to the place that he had hoped, in time, he might call home.

From the headland, he had seen, in the distance, Rick's cab from the nearest town pull up at his cottage. He knew who his visitor was and laughed out loud at the fact that the last person he wanted to see was the only person to have bothered to travel so far into the bleakness of winter.

Her hair was white now, stripped of all the fabulous colours of their youth. Her back was no longer straight and her fingers, heavy with rings, bent in time to resemble something like the talons of the seabirds he watched every day. Her journey must have been important to her, he thought. She hated flying and she hated boats.

'Conrad's dead,' she said, as he stood there, filling the tiny doorway, watching her sitting at his plain wooden table, clutching a mug of tea she must have made herself, helping herself to his kitchen with an easy familiarity or perhaps some proprietorial sense that made the man uncomfortable.

She had no bags with her, and he had no telephone. He hoped that she had arranged for Rick to come back and pick her up at some point soon. The town was half an hour away on bad roads and from there she could get a bus back to the capital.

'Conrad's dead,' she repeated, softer, more quietly, so that, with the wind and surf behind him, the words were swept into the dark corners of the cottage. He nodded once, slowly, and then turned his back to look at the birds wheeling on the wind, their song harsh and mocking.

He didn't want her, of all people, to the see the tear that had formed in the corner of his eye and was threatening to run down his wind-reddened cheek to settle in his salt-stiffened beard. If she knew where he lived, she could have sent him a letter care of the Post Office in town, old school, poste restante.

It had been a different lifetime then, back when the woman was not much more than a girl and he was not much more than a boy, really, with a soft curly beard that his mother called 'bum fluff', and there, with them, was Conrad. The three of them lived in a rented ramshackle house in the shade of the floating dock on one side and the grey concrete wheat silos on the other. They were pretending to be students and talked about how they would be friends forever and how nothing would ever tear them apart, and now, she had come to confirm that they were irrevocably torn asunder, as he, more than anyone, knew. The fact that Conrad was dead was, to the man, just a sad footnote on something that really ended a long time ago.

'How?' he asked.

She did not answer and just sat, twisting the rings on her fingers.

He had often thought about both of them, Conrad and the woman who was now sitting at his table, and wondered how time might have treated them and if they were still together and if they had found the peace that he never could. He remembered that time he had walked out of the house in the shadow of the wheat silo that one last time, that sultry night when the mingled wheat dust and coal dust stuck to his skin, when the sweat ran in rivers down his back, the sobs of the woman in his ears—confessions and recriminations heavy in the shadow cast by the one weak light post in the narrow street where a lot of things could stay hidden, the truth not being the least.

'I came because I have a question,' the woman said.

'And you think that I might have an answer?' the man said from the doorway, unable to enter his own home for reasons he did not quite understand. The woman sat quite still, looking at the tabletop, continuing to fiddle with her rings.

'I think that I deserve it,' she said slowly and deliberately. The man turned and looked around the fields leading to the cliff, hoping that the cold water would rise up and take him like some barely imagined biblical tale where he could be washed clean and redeemed by the Southern Ocean.

47

'That night…' the woman said and paused, and the man knew without her needing to say anything more what night she meant.

'That night,' the man said.

'When you left us.'

In the way that he had rewritten the past in his own mind, the man liked to think that he had walked purposefully to the end of the street, turned and crossed the bridge over the creek where the fishing trawlers tied up, and continued walking down to the railway station where, duffle bag over his shoulder, he had boarded the train to the city. He knew that, as much as he liked that version of events, it was not true and that he had hesitated, waiting under the weak streetlight where he could be seen, hoping that the woman or Conrad or both of them would come after him and ask him to return and to stay but they never did.

'And now he's dead,' the man said, 'and now it's over?'

'You chose him over me,' the woman said, looking for the first time into the man's eyes.

'And he chose you over everybody,' the man said, and the woman looked away again.

'Why here? Why did you come to this place?' the woman asked.

'Because at night, when there is no fog or cloud, you can really see the stars and sometimes the lights, the borealis, and it makes you feel unimportant amongst all that vastness,' the man said, knowing that the words were as true as any he could have chosen to use without telling the full story.

They both remained where they were, he in the doorway, she in the chair, and he was surprised at how, in the beginning, years before, he had hoped that they would come looking for him, first in the city and then the other cities and towns, always heading further south, and then, in time, he began to fear them coming, digging up old pains. But now she had finally found him, he felt nothing and the emptiness scared him more than anything, more than the stars and the big southern night sky.

He heard a sound from down the track and, turning, he saw that it was Rick's cab making its way along the narrow roadway and realised that the woman must have asked Rick to come back at a certain time.

'My taxi?' she asked. The man nodded. The woman looked at him and raised an eyebrow waiting for him to answer the unanswered question and he shrugged his shoulder as he watched the taxi negotiate its way up the hill.

'I expected as much,' the woman said. The man looked at her in puzzlement. 'Your silence,' she said, 'that's what I expected.' And the man thought that there was a tear in her eye that wasn't from the salty sea air or the lingering peat smoke in the air.

The woman stood up and placed a small canvas carry bag on the table bearing the name of a major supermarket chain. From the bag, she pulled out a largish aluminium jar with a screw top lid and placed it down on the opposite side of the table from where she had been sitting. She made no comment about the jar but softly excused herself and the man stood aside so that the woman could pass through the narrow doorway to the taxi that had arrived and was parked a few metres away, it's engine running. The man looked at the jar and back at the woman.

'I've brought him to you. He always talked about this place and about wanting to come here and visit one day. You can be together at last, just the two of you, the way you both really wanted it to be.' The woman didn't say another word and, as the taxi carried her away, she never looked back.

Pigboy on the Train

Shea J Evans

Local Award

The doors of the nine o'clock morning train out of Grafton slid shut, and Pigboy sniffed through its carriages in search of an unoccupied place to settle. It was a small train, with only a handful aboard, so Pigboy was able to find his spot with relative ease. He adjusted his rucksack as he entered the empty car, and slung the bag onto an aisle seat as he slid up against the window with his shoulder. He rested his head on the glass and closed his eyes. Behind him now were the bridges, one new, and one old, that spanned the Clarence just upstream of where it forked around Susan Island.

Behind him was what he had always, until today, thought of as being his side of town. Behind him now were a lot of things. He tried to think of the river, with its life and its cycles, but shuddered at his knowledge of its other secrets.

There was a shrill whistle, and the train shunted forward on its long lurch. Pigboy's forehead skittered across the glass. He straightened in his seat and opened his eyes. Standing in the aisle of the otherwise lonely carriage, staring at Pigboy, was an old man.

'What?' asked Pigboy.

The old man took this as an invitation to step closer. 'Don't worry,' he said. 'I'm not the inspector.'

Pigboy shuddered. It was clear that the man, with his torn flannel shirt, sun-bleached hat, and unkempt white beard, was no inspector. Over his shoulder was a rucksack, much like Pigboy's.

The old man nodded at the pair of empty seats facing Pigboy. 'These taken?'

'No,' said Pigboy, who was not a liar.

'Might park here, then,' he said. He eased himself into the aisle seat and set his bag against the window. 'I'm Jesper.'

Pigboy just nodded.

'Well,' said Jesper. 'Where you headed?'

'South,' said Pigboy.

'I can see that. I know how the train runs.'

'I'm headed south,' said Pigboy.

'Ah,' said Jesper. 'It's like that. Is it that you don't know, or you won't say?'

Pigboy blinked. He didn't want the old man to think he was stupid or unwanted.

'I'm going to Newcastle. I'm staying with a cousin.'

Jesper laughed. 'We've all got a cousin or two in Newcastle, don't we? They dry up, quick enough. Are you running from something? Someone?'

Pigboy's head swivelled on his neck and he looked through the old man's face.

'No.'

Jesper laughed again. 'Been there, matey,' he said. 'All running from something, aren't we? Don't worry, I won't be in your hair long. Only on the line 'til Coffs.'

Pigboy grunted. He turned back to the window. Out of it was a montage, like an old eight-mil reel show of the cheapest, most dilapidated houses and backyards in South Grafton, the ones on the close side of the tracks. He saw sagging trampolines being dragged down to earth by overgrown lawns and weeds a metre high. He saw smashed concrete and broken glass, boarded up shed windows and doors half hanging on like the teeth of so many neglected children. He saw rusted swings and playsets, and forgotten, raggedy palm trees, fronds decomposing on their trunks, as well as a car with yellow graffiti sprayed quickly all over it. *Fuck you, pEdoFile rokspider basterd.*

A shuffling movement from the opposite seat caught Pigboy's attention. When he looked over to Jesper, he saw that the old man had half removed a brown paper bag from the rucksack beside him. Jesper's eyes were on Pigboy's face, and it took a moment for him to realise. When he looked into the eyes of the old man he felt the pull of something intimate and familiar, of some kindred but unspeakable nature. An overlapping spark.

'You mind a drink?' asked Jesper.

It was unclear whether the old man was enquiring as to the status of Pigboy's own desire to drink, which was always strong, or whether he was sifting for any objection that Pigboy might harbour if forced to witness a stranger drink by himself on the train. In order to allow the old man's vice, without cutting off his own access to it, Pigboy said:

'I don't mind one at all.'

Jesper grinned, like a fox, and a certain electricity arced in his eye. He looked around the car, and when he had ascertained that they were alone he pulled the bottle out and unscrewed the cap. He took a deep swig and let out a satisfied sound that was half moan and half sigh. The old man wiped his mouth with his sleeve and proffered the bottle to Pigboy. Pigboy looked, wary, at Jesper, and at the bottle held in the air between them.

'Fancy a snort?' asked the old man.

Pigboy's ears pricked up. 'A snort?'

Here Jesper held his laughter, but allowed a smirk to drift across his face. 'Now that says a lot about a young man,' he said, shaking the bottle. 'A snort once meant a swig.'

'Oh.'

Pigboy reached out and took the bottle from the old man. He didn't check to see what it was, just raised it to his lips. A shock of Irish whiskey flowed between his teeth.

'Jameson?' asked Pigboy. He handed the bottle back to Jesper and wiped his own mouth.

'Tullamore Dew,' said the old man, then, nodding at the thongs on Pigboy's feet: 'Have you got a good pair of steelcaps, then?'

Pigboy tried not to react. Talk of boots, when one is wearing open rubber, will chafe a person like that. 'In my bag I do, certainly.'

'Good,' said Jesper. 'There's always need of a man with a good pair of boots on his feet. And speaking of feet, never forget you were born with two.'

Pigboy looked closely at the old man. 'I won't,' he said. His travelling companion seemed more open now, and, if Pigboy was being honest, he felt more open himself. 'Thanks, by the way. For the snort.'

'Not a worry,' said Jesper. 'Better to have and to share, than to have and to hold.'

'Generosity makes the world go round,' said Pigboy, and a grin formed on his own face.

The old man removed the hat from his head and revealed an oily, liver-spotted pate. He took another snort of Dew and handed it back to Pigboy. 'Truer words were never spoken,' he said. 'You have to know when to give, and when to take.'

'Oh,' said Pigboy, imbibing another draught. 'No doubt about it.'

Pigboy felt bile rise in the upper parts of his stomach, diaphragm and throat as the drink sought its harsh path through to the ends of him. He cradled the bottle between his knees and looked back through the window, so that the sights thereout might settle his spirit. They had left most of town behind, and now the scenery was defined by the kinds of plants that grow close to the rail line in such latitudes. Pigboy saw ferns, vines, morning glory, a tangle of things all striving for dominance, and native tobaccos, like coral atolls, punching above the slew. Here and there were the odd jacaranda and camphor laurel, diminutive, juvenile outcasts that would be choked out by the creeping greenery before their first flowerings. Such a place ate the tall and shallow-rooted. Pigboy turned back to Jesper and passed the whiskey.

'So,' he said. 'What's in Coffs?'

The old man propped the bottle between his own knees and rubbed at his face with both hands, which Pigboy was afforded a moment's observation of. They were huge hands, huge, like the rest of the man, Pigboy now saw, and had attained the level of angry, red, calloused scarification that hands can only achieve after years of gloveless use. Jesper pulled the hat back onto his head.

'I have some business to attend,' he said.

'Oh,' said Pigboy, emboldened by Jesper's gift. 'What sort of business?'

The old man's face darkened. 'Something that needs seeing to.'

A beat of understanding pulsed through Pigboy. He made a choice to enquire no further, which the old man recognised and was pleased by.

'And also,' he said, smirking. 'There's a woman I know there who'll do anything after a bottle of Jim Beam.'

Pigboy laughed and winked and said, 'Well, that sounds like a decent sort of show.' But inside he winced. The image of the old bushie and his local lizard did not inspire much joy, and Pigboy found this new level of openness distasteful. He checked the time on his phone.

'I'd say we're not far off Coffs Harbour, now.'

Jesper looked out the window. 'Still a few turns yet,' he said, and drank from the bottle. Pigboy, of course, was obliged to accept another swallow when offered.

There was a period of comfortable silence. Then, as if in response to something that had just transpired, the old man let out a long and sad exhalation.

'It's a hard life, isn't it?' he asked Pigboy.

'From what I've seen so far,' he said.

Jesper snorted. 'You've seen a bit of it, I can tell,' he said. 'But you haven't seen the half of it. As you get older…'

Pigboy had met a few old men before, so he waited for what might come next. But there was nothing, apart from a heaviness that had settled over the carriage. Pigboy made to dispel it.

'Some have it harder than others,' he said.

Jesper nodded along, his lips pursed, eyebrows raised. 'Technically true.'

'And some have it better,' said Pigboy.

At this the old man let out an approving scoff, and his nodding became as though directed at somebody else. 'Very true,' he said.

'But we all have something.'

Jesper leaned back in his seat and closed his eyes. His head became still, and a gentle smile creased the corners of his mouth. Then he whispered Pigboy's words back to himself. *'But we all have something.'*

The train made an obvious deceleration as he said this. The old man opened his eyes and looked at Pigboy.

'Well,' he said. 'That sounds like me.'

Jesper stood up to exit the train. He gathered his pack around himself and extended his hand. For a moment Pigboy thought it was an invitation to shake. Then he saw that the old man was offering him the brown bag and its contents.

'Here you go,' he said. 'It's a long way to Tipperary, and I've got to find some Jimmy.'

Pigboy accepted his gift with outward thanks and inward amusement. He enjoyed meeting people like Jesper; they were a good distraction. At the very least they were a bit of entertainment. He saluted the old man.

'Good luck out there, soldier,' he said.

The old man touched the brim of his hat. 'Back at you, Captain,' he said. 'And remember—if you can't be good, be good at it.'

Then he wandered away, and only looked over his shoulder at Pigboy once.

Then Pigboy was alone again, and he watched a few people step off the train and onto the platform. He looked for Jesper, but he was gone. Instead, he sat and pondered the old man's adage over another swig of Dew. *Be good*, he thought. *Or be good at it.* There was another whistle, and the train pulled away in search of its momentum. Pigboy checked his phone again and sighed. He shifted in his seat and considered the bottle that Jesper had just given him. Then he unzipped his rucksack and considered the one he had packed the day prior in anticipation of the journey. It was a long way to Newcastle.

At least he wouldn't be bored.

Earthquake Correspondents

Garry Jennings

Local Award

On 28 December 1989 at 10:27am, an earthquake measuring 5.6 on the Richter scale hit Newcastle. The earthquake caused 13 fatalities and 160 people were injured. The impact on infrastructure, property and relationships was widespread.

**

Newcastle, January 1990

Bolton Point 2283

Dear Ms/Sir

Please place the following advertisement in the Personals Section (Men Seeking Women) of the next edition of The Newcastle Star and invoice me at the above address:

Educated guy in early thirties, a lapsed Anglican with usual hang-ups and divorced with one child, seeks progressive, warm-to-hot woman to 40 years, with whom to share post-earthquake trauma in Newcastle. Ideally should have conversational range from Big Macs to brown rice and never have watched Dynasty. *Children OK. Sydney TV not essential. All letters answered.*

Sincerely,
Brian Nancarrow

New Lambton 2305

My dear sir!

I wish to apply for the advertised position of 'post-earthquake' female companion. I seem to fulfil most of your criteria, and although I do not have Sydney TV reception, I only ever watch the ABC.

I am blessed with the 'usual hang-ups', too, but they will fade away when I resign soon from a Lake Macquarie high school where I have been one of the 'zoo keepers' for far too long. And while I can proudly declare that I have never watched *Dynasty*, I HAVE been to the Palais Royale on a 'ladies night'—but only in the interests of broadening my conversational range, you understand.

Incidentally, my own earthquake trauma resulted from being ripped off to the tune of $600 by a couple of ambulance chasing cowboys who pulled my teetering chimneys down the day after the tremor. I know the insurance company pays, but it's still annoying, isn't it?

Now I don't normally do things like this but my girlfriends have forced me (!) to put pen to paper because they're sick of my turning up to their dinner parties alone. I hope that my 'application' will be considered favourably. Should you wish to contact me for an 'interview', you can phone me on XXXXXX. If you show me your earthquake damage, then I'll show you mine.

Tess

Edgeworth 2285

Dear Mr Big Macs and Brown Rice Man

I am a Filipina woman of 28 years and am writing to offer myself to comfort your sorrow after your terrible earthquake. I live in a village on Cebu Island in the Philippines and would very much like to be your wife in Newcastle. I received the newspaper address from my cousin, Lilian, who is living in
Edgeworth, near your city. I see the photos of your Workers Club Cathedral and where the roof fall down and it is terrible thing. I never

watch *Dynasty* TV show here but I like very much Mork and Mindy. If you send me money and air ticket I will be your good wife. I send you photo of me in traditional dress at my nephew's baptism. Send letter to my cousin Lilian in Edgeworth.

Yours in God's name
Nellie Mendoza

Redhead 2290

Dear Guy

In reply to your ad in this week's Star, may I present to you my curriculum vitae: **Name**: Annaliese **Age**: 29 (in this life) **Build**: Slim! (from eating lots of brown rice!) **Star Sign**: Pisces (with Aries cusp) **Hair**: Naturally blonde and shoulder length **Parental Status**: One precocious six-year-old boy **Hobbies**: Body-building, weightlifting, hockey and sewing (that last one made you sit up, I bet) **Occupation**: Picture-framer, gardener, mother (!#?) **Domicile**: At the moment, I'm in limbo. I'm living in Redhead Caravan Park among earthquake reffos and heaps of guys from Parents without Partners because, some Nazi from the council has plastered my poor house with red stickers and roped it off with orange plastic tape because it's 'unsafe' **Conversational Range**: Anything from Nimbin and mud-bricks to Mrs Knebel Kitchens.

Also, I'm SO 'progressive' that I don't even own a TV. But I do need a few laughs. Feel free to write to me c/-PO Box Redhead 2290.

Hope to hear from you, 'educated guy'!
Annaliese

Wickham 2276

Dear Man

I'm sorry to confess that I have watched *Dynasty* a few times. That's the bad news. The good news is that I'm a warm (occasionally hot) woman in my early thirties. 'Progressive? Mmm, I usually associate that with barn dancing but I do feel that I can run with most ideas (though I'm not sure my children would agree!)

59

Our household has been in turmoil lately. My husband and I have separated but when an awning collapsed on him in Beaumont St during the earthquake, he came back here to recuperate (only temporarily, of course!)

I hope you won't mind talking about your OWN credentials for embarking on a relationship. I, too, am badly in need of some decent conversation, so call me on XXXXXX But please hang up if a man answers. For the purposes of this letter, and for now, I'm known as Fran.

Jewellstown 2280

Dear Whoever

I didn't understand most of your ad, but I'm very curious so I thought I'd write to you anyway. You sound as pissed off as I am just now. What is there to do in this shithole of a town now? The Workers Club's collapsed, they've pulled down the City RSL and where are the nightclubs? There's no way Fannys'll open again anytime soon. It beats me how you would survive these days without Sydney TV reception. Anyway, down to the nitty gritty, eh?

I'm 31, single, train German Shepherds and supervise the evening shift at Broadmeadow Sizzler. Life's been pretty hectic lately, to say the least. One of my dogs got knocked on the head by a brick that the quake shook off the back wall. I've been nursing her at home but the vet's fees are really killing me.

I give dog obedience training classes down at Hillsborough on Sunday morning from 10am. Call me on XXXXXX at Sizzler or come down to dog training this weekend. Just ask for Judy.

P.S. Hope you like dogs

My Dear Son

I was greatly moved on reading your advertisement in the local paper and pray that this letter reaches you. Did I recognise a plea for help and understanding in your short entreaty, nestled tragically among other sad and desperate pleas from prostitutes and other deviates? You confess to having strayed from the dogma of the Church of England. Perhaps the upheaval in your life, exacerbated by this earthquake, is the Lord's way of guiding you towards a new flock? Your criticism of the shallow nature of today's television is certainly well founded. It will obviously be a dangerous influence on your own child, probably already damaged by the trauma of divorce. Don't hesitate to phone me on the above number at any hour. Your despair will be our joyful burden.

In God's name
(Father) Patrick Pringle

Eleebana 2282

Brian? Seriously? Brian?

Big Macs to brown rice?? Are you fair dinkum, mate? How much do you think you can get away with in this town? It may have struck gold the first time you advertised. That's how you and Julia got together, after all. Why didn't you just include your name address and business card with this one? Mate, you'd do just as well to try your luck at The Brewery on Friday nights on the front line with me. I must admit, though, that the old town is pretty dead. Quietest New Year's Eve, I've ever seen.

I was really sorry to hear about your house, mate. How long before the assessors go over it? Give me a call at work, for God's sake. It's hard to track you down now that you're home phone is cactus. Hang in there and remember your mates if you're landed with more women than you can handle.

Take care
Dougie

Dear Brian (don't worry, I know it's you)

I can see you've got nothing better to do since the earthquake than sit around and write your loony 'lonely hearts' letters to The Star. As your honorary ex-wife, I could certainly enlighten any woman who is silly enough to reply what she'd be getting herself into.

I think it's so infantile of you to go on with this rubbish about watching *Dynasty*. You watched your fair share of twaddle on SBS when we were together and I don't appreciate such a cheap shot at me.

I've had to cope with a lot since the damn earthquake too. Sally's bottom came up in a big bruise after the tremor bumped her off the slippery dip in the Maccas playground. And not that it's a big deal, but she's still wound up that the girl at the counter wouldn't sell us an egg McMuffin because the power had gone off and breakfast finished at 10.30.

She's worried that her doll's house was damaged when your roof fell in, too. I know she can't stay with you where you are now, but you could at least take her out for a day on the weekends. I need a break too. And you still owe for a fortnight's maintenance.

Happy courting, Lover Boy.

Susie

Cooks Hill 2300

Dear Brian

I have a horrible, aching feeling that you (or someone who sounds awfully like you) may have advertised recently in the Star's personal columns. Let's not kid ourselves that we don't still read them. But anyway, I want to put that aside because there are some things I need to get off my chest.

I think we made a mistake in not talking things through fully the last time. And now it's such a friggin' hassle getting into and out of Stalag Cooks Hill through the barricades that I simply don't have the energy to visit you at your 'Lake Retreat'.

The shock has only just registered. No pun intended. I can't believe how lucky it was that Jake wasn't at school when it happened. The main teaching block there is such a mess.

I don't think we can continue to put our relationship (if that's what it is) on hold while we wait for all this chaos to subside. Do you want to know what I've been doing since the 28th?…vacuuming up earthquake dust all day, and nursing the kids through asthma attacks at night. I couldn't find Jake's puffer anywhere last night and nearly went hysterical while he was gasping for air.

I know you've got a lot to deal with. You've probably hardly seen Sally for ages and she'll be missing you like crazy. But god, I miss you too, damn it! We're actually good together, Brian, if you didn't realise that. The relationship doesn't have to go on the line just because we both get the shits occasionally.

It must be such a drag for you (ha ha) now staying with someone whose Richter Scale is rocked by watching Sale of the Century. You're such a middle class wanker, you know. Having trouble getting SBS out there, are you? OK. I've said what I wanted to, so I'll leave it there. Look after yourself. Ring me. I won't hassle you again, promise.

Love,
Julia

Cooks Hill 2300

Dear Ms/Sir

Please place the following advertisement in the Personals Section of the next edition of The Star and invoice me at the changed address above.

Educated guy in early thirties, a lapsed Anglican with usual hang-ups and divorced etc etc, who placed this ad two weeks ago, wishes to thank all those who replied. Now unable to answer all letters personally due to rebuilding after earthquake.

Brian Nancarrow

Cosmic Latte

Michael Tippett

Local Award

Alan Manning stood perfectly straight behind the counter of Paymart's Home Entertainment Department. A fluorescent panel flickered overhead, and he blinked at the twitchy light. His controller—the gelatinous octopoid suctioned to his head—blinked in unison. He sipped a latte and scanned the rows of movies, music, and other media arranged in immaculate order.

'Good morning, Alan Manning.' Assistant Manager Dennis Fetch stepped in front of a display model video camera. His pasty, middle-aged face filled the wall of televisions behind Alan. 'Company policy forbids the consumption of refreshments outside of scheduled breaks.' Dennis's controller clenched a tentacle. Its egg-shaped cranium inflated, and internal organs bulged beneath translucent skin.

'This body is not adapted to night shift,' Alan said. 'Caffeine stimulates the central nervous system and enhances performance.'

'Unacceptable.' Dennis lifted a handset. His flawless monotone echoed over the public address system. 'Code 67 in Home Entertainment.' He returned the handset and straightened his name badge. 'Descension Day sales begin in 48 hours. Paymart cannot risk any deviations from its code of conduct.'

'I apologise, Dennis Fetch.' Alan glanced at his watch. 'My shift concluded three minutes ago. Judy Wong is late.'

'It is my reason for greeting you this morning. Judy Wong is afflicted with involuntary bowel movements. You are required to perform her shift. Do you comply?'

A security guard walked past and swiped the latte from Alan's hand.

'I repeat,' Dennis said, 'do you comply?'

Alan looked down at his empty grip. 'I comply.'

Clusters of people navigated the street in synchronised steps, their octopoid controllers bobbing up and down. Alan Manning broke from the crowd and entered his apartment building. A cleaner occupied the foyer, scrubbing the spray-painted words 'Free the Jellyheads' off a tiled wall.

Alan shuffled into the elevator and pressed the button for the eighth floor.

A woman guided a large blank canvas through the building entrance. 'Please delay your ascent,' she said.

Alan held the doors until she stepped inside. The elevator rattled on its way upwards. Neurons activated in his host's brain and a memory surfaced. 'You are Claire Perkins,' he said.

'Correct. And you are Alan Manning from the apartment opposite mine.'

'That is correct. I have not seen you for some time.'

'I am newly merged,' Claire said. 'My host fled after the Descension. She operated with the Human Resistance until her recent subjugation.'

Another memory triggered in Alan. 'We engaged in sexual intercourse on one occasion.'

Claire nodded. 'During a night of excessive alcohol consumption. My host's impaired judgement misconstrued your desperation as an attractive characteristic. She failed to respond to any of your text messages afterwards. I understand she even utilised the fire escape to avoid meeting your host in the hallway.'

'He suspected as much,' Alan said.

The elevator lurched and opened with a ping.

Alan and Claire moved along the hallway, stopping at their respective doors. Mozart's *Requiem* floated from further down.

'Peculiar,' Alan said. 'That sound is originating from Harold Keeley's apartment.'

'His host was a piano teacher. Perhaps he is questioning why a human would commit their life to something as impractical as music?' Claire opened her door. 'I must expel urine. Good night, Alan Manning.'

He watched her vanish inside her apartment. 'Good night, Claire Perkins.'

Alan sat in his armchair, a half-eaten microwave dinner on his lap. The empty glow of the television shed the only light in the room. He flicked through channels and snippets of news reports flashed onscreen.

'—Descension Day anniversary will commemorate twelve months since the conquest of Earth. Organisers are—'

'—concerns of a weaponised empathogen. The Human Resistance has yet to claim responsibility, but authorities—'

'—if you suspect someone is contaminated with an emotion, contact the hotline on—'

Alan muted the television. He stifled a yawn and placed the dinner tray on a side table. His controller quivered. Its bulbous eyes drooped until they finally closed.

Alan woke to muffled shouts in the middle of the night. He stood and opened his front door. Classical music blared through the hallway. Four men in hazmat suits—their helmets disproportionately large to accommodate their controllers—wheeled Harold Keeley away on a gurney. Harold fought his restraints and ranted under a gag. His octopoid's fleshy tentacles whipped about, pulsing with an intense violet light.

The music ceased and a fifth man in a hazmat suit emerged from Harold's apartment.

'Is Harold Keeley unwell?' Alan asked.

The man approached. He produced a book from a belt pouch. 'Have you had recent interaction with your neighbour, citizen?'

'I greet him in the hallway on occasion, but we have not—'

'Prepare for screening.' The man opened the book to a random page. Alan spotted the title on the cover: *The World's Funniest Joke Book*. 'Are you ready to commence?'

'I am,' Alan said.

The man cleared his throat and read aloud. 'Did you hear about the kidnapping at school?'

'I did not.'

'*He woke up.*'

Alan blinked and waited. 'Has the joke concluded?'

'Yes,' the man said. 'Are you experiencing a reaction? The contraction of facial muscles or an inclination to slap your thigh?'

'I am not,' Alan said. 'Are you certain this joke would influence someone burdened with a sense of humour? Its function seems questionable.'

'Perhaps an alternate method of screening? A percussive examination?'

'What is a percuss—' The punch struck Alan in the face. Blood trickled from his nose, and he wiped it with the back of a hand.

'No indication of pain response,' the man said. 'You are clear, citizen. Good evening.'

Alan watched him leave. Claire slipped out of her door in a dressing gown.

'You are injured,' she said.

'My controller is unharmed. It is all that matters.'

'If your body bleeds out, you will have nothing to control. Allow me to administer aid.'

Alan considered her words. 'I will allow it,' he said.

The apartment was similar in design to Alan's but not nearly as orderly. Art supplies and mismatched furniture cluttered the space. Paintings rested along the walls. A drop sheet shielded a section of floor.

Claire dipped a swab in antiseptic solution and applied it to Alan's inflamed nostrils. 'It does not appear broken,' she said.

Alan surveyed the room. 'Why do most of these paintings contain your host's face?'

'Self-portraits. A puzzling trend. Humans develop eyes to see outside of themselves, yet they spend most of their time looking back in.'

'There are many aspects of their behaviour I do not understand,' Alan said. 'For instance, why do they resist us? We offer a world without pain, without war. A society free of religious and political divides. Yet the remaining pockets of unmerged humans continue to oppose us. It baffles the mind.'

Claire smoothed a nasal strip across Alan's nose. 'This will promote breathing until the swelling subsides. I have completed my aid.'

Alan stepped around her. He approached the large canvas on an easel next to a window. A rough coat of pale-yellow paint covered most of the canvas. 'What is this?'

'A work in progress.' She moved to stand beside him. 'My host was an artist. Even though I do not understand the purpose of art, it is important to maintain human endeavours if we are to assimilate their society.'

'A portrait of the colour yellow?'

'FFF8E7 to be precise. In the RGB model it is comprised of 100% red,

97.25% green, and 90.59% blue. The humans named it Cosmic Latte.'

'Cosmic Latte?'

'Correct. In 2002, Earth scientists determined it to be the average colour of the universe. If you were to condense existence into a single image, this is how it would appear.'

'It seems logical,' Alan said.

'In what respect?'

He leaned in for a closer look. 'That our world would be beige.'

Dennis Fetch dropped a folder on Alan's counter. 'Paymart is implementing new censorship regulations. This stock must be removed immediately.'

Alan opened the folder and skimmed over the list of titles. '*E.T. the Extra-Terrestrial. Inside Out. The Notebook.* The first ten minutes of *Up*?' He looked at the assistant manager. 'Dennis Fetch, how do I remove a section of—'

'Music is being recalled as well. Any albums that could elicit an emotional response.'

'Would that not be all of them?'

Dennis nodded. 'Everything except for Coldplay, Dave Matthews Band, and the artist referred to as Sting.' He adjusted the belt on his impeccably ironed trousers. 'Descension Day sales start tomorrow. You will clear this stock off the shelves before your shift is concluded. Do you comply?'

Alan gripped the folder. His controller released a warbled hiss from its beak-like mouth. 'I…comply.'

Sirens wailed in the distance. Alan caught a streak of violet light disappearing into an alley. He entered his building and rode the elevator to the eighth floor. Claire's door was open. The lights were off within.

'Claire?' Alan leaned through her doorway. 'Are you present?' He stepped inside and his eyes adjusted to the gloom. Paintings, torn and smashed, were strewn about the apartment. The only artwork left untouched was the large canvas near the window.

Alan took out his phone and found Claire's number. It rang for several moments before she answered.

'H-hello?' Her voice sounded frail, strange.

'Claire, what is the matter? You have left your apartment in a state of disarray. I would avoid entertaining guests until it is resolved.'

'Alan, I am unwell. My mind is racing with so many thoughts. I am… frightened.'

'Frightened? You require immediate assistance. Where are you located? I will contact the authorities and—'

'No!' The intensity of the word caused Alan's controller to clamp down on his head. 'You cannot comprehend the freedom I am experiencing in this moment. I see the truth of the world we have inherited. And would you like to know a secret, Alan Manning? *It is not beige.* It is breathtakingly beautiful and heartbreakingly ugly, and I would not have it any other way. I will not be controlled any longer…'

'Claire, you must listen to my words. This is not—'

'They will come for me. I must go. Please be well.'

The phone went dead.

Alan pondered in the darkness. The stink of turpentine cloyed the air. He switched on a light, exposing the chaos in the room. Alan approached the large canvas and gazed at the finished work. A perfect rectangle of pale-yellow paint. His fingers traced grooves on the drying canvas, and he realised this was more than a simple colour. It was a doorway—a portal. Time lost its rhythm. The painting unravelled around him, and he witnessed quasars and comets and blackholes—the sum of all existence in the strokes of a brush. Neurons flared in Alan's brain and the octopoid controller shuddered. His universe expanded at the speed of thought, and he was suddenly aware of a dull ache in his nose.

'Did you hear about the kidnapping at school?' he muttered to himself.

Clusters of people packed into the store. Paymart employees herded them, like cattle, from bargain to bargain. There was no panic, no hysteria, only committed shoppers seeking to part with their money.

Alan stood behind the counter of the Home Entertainment Department. He waited for the store to reach capacity and lifted the handset. His voice rang over the public address system. 'Attention, consumers. We have a surprise in Home Entertainment for our Paymart shoppers. Please proceed to the counter to claim your once-in-a-lifetime gift.'

The crowd swelled. Dennis Fetch tried to force his way through but failed. His voice drowned amongst the throng. 'I did not authorise a gift,

Alan Manning. You will comply!'

Alan reached over the counter. He pulled the sheet from the object positioned in front of the video camera. Cosmic Latte filled the wall of televisions behind him.

'What is it?' a shopper asked.

Alan found his smile. 'Yours.'

Chrysalis: the aftermath

Michelle Haines Thomas

I leave the porch light on and sit for hours on the other side of the screen door.

I try not to stare directly at it the whole time, but still find myself occasionally mesmerised, just like the insects. The globe-shaped cover leaves blue sunspots in my field of vision when I move my eyes away. I'm waiting for my moth to come back.

Misty, my border collie, waits with me, and shifts incrementally closer to me every now and then until she is well and truly sitting on my foot.

I am neither hot nor cold, tired nor alert, hungry nor sated. I am just waiting, in something like a state of suspended animation, sitting in a hard, wooden chair and watching the light out of the corner of my eye.

It is quiet.

I've done the same thing for two nights in a row, ever since Sam up and left.

He was, as I've come to recognise, in a manic phase and had been building a head of steam all week.

'Mum! You're not listening to me!' he shouted that night, slamming his hands on the kitchen table. 'I've thought of everything. It's a perfect plan—I just need that money and then I can make it happen. Do you want me to miss my chance?'

He wanted my savings to start a food van—hotdogs to be precise. He had a plan to sell them at markets, country shows, maybe the odd quirky wedding or event. The food van was listed on a Facebook group and cost $8000.

It wasn't a bad idea, especially compared to some of the others he'd come up with since leaving school, but the problem wasn't the idea, really. It was Sam. It is Sam.

Sam, who got expelled from three different high schools. Sam, who's been arrested twice for assault. Sam, who can't sit still long enough to watch a movie on the couch. My Sam, my only child, my baby, who charmed us all with his sweetness and mischief, who lives his adult life oscillating between delight and despair.

He'd been as intrigued as I was earlier in the week. After a storm, I'd gone outside to sweep up the mess on the back porch and, under the table, I saw a shape among the leaves. Dark brown, as long as my little finger, almost like a slender nut or seed. I reached down to pick it up and dropped it immediately when it moved between my fingers.

One end of the cocoon—because I could see now that's what it was—had twirled at my touch.

I picked it up again and rested it on my palm. The casing was hard and heavy, with half of it solid and immovable. But the other end, now swivelling urgently, was grub-like in shape with armoured bands that allowed the creature inside to flex. It had a tiny thread protruding from the top that I supposed had once allowed it to hang somewhere, perhaps under my outdoor table.

I'd called Sam over to show him the strange dancing chrysalis, and he'd held it himself and looked at me in astonishment, laughing. Misty came over to sniff at the shape, but was uninterested and moved on to do a wee in the rock garden.

I found an old vase and taped the fibre to the inside of the clear glass, then covered the top of it with a mesh strainer. I put it on the kitchen bench where I could keep an eye on it. It had everything it needed—light and air and safety. And when the pupa emerged, transformed, I could examine it. Then I'd let it go.

I was desperate to see what came out. I suspected it was a moth of some kind, and I did a reverse image search on Google so I could narrow down the type. Maybe a hawk moth? Or something called a bastilla?

The chrysalis sat on the bench in its vase for two days. I talked to it as I cooked dinner for Sam and me, and when I got a glass of water, and when I made tea. I moved it next to my computer while I worked on a website update. It was strangely good company, calm and consistent. I looked at it closely each day to see if there was any sign of change, but there was nothing.

Meanwhile, Sam came and went, not always to the place he was meant to come and go from. He begged off a shift at Coles because he wasn't feeling up to it, then spent the day at the beach, and later at a friend's place. He walked in at midnight, his eyes unnaturally bright and his energy high.

The next day he worked but left early because he had to go to the doctor. This was legitimate—he did go to the doctor—but I can imagine what his boss thought. Why would they keep him around when there were reliable people lining up for work? This would be another job he couldn't stick at, another—and I'd never say this word to him, but it beat like a drum in my head—failure. When would he change? Would he ever?

He came back from the doctor all revved up. He had a new mental health plan and a referral to a new psychiatrist. This was going to work this time. He was going to follow through with all his appointments and take whatever meds he was prescribed. He was going to get his act together and make a plan.

He began sorting through his wardrobe, as if his chaotic jumble of clothes had been the problem all along. Then he stopped and wrote down a meal plan for the week, following a keto diet, presenting it to me with an insistence that we needed to buy more and better meat. I disagreed, being vegetarian. Also, we couldn't afford it. He told me I was holding him back, and didn't I want him to succeed in life? Then he sat down with a beer and flicked through Facebook, looking on the local classifieds group—he'd been searching for hand weights so he could work out in the garage. That's when he found the food van and had his eureka moment.

He did some frantic sums on the back of an envelope. I watched him at the table from where I was cutting up carrots at the kitchen bench. I had put the vase containing the chrysalis on the table out of the way, the mesh strainer still balanced over the wide glass mouth. Misty sat on the floor, hoping for scraps even though I was only cutting vegetables.

Sam scribbled and talked to himself a bit before he looked up triumphantly.

'Mum, you're never going to believe what I've found.'

It escalated quickly from there. I suggested caution, making a business plan, talking to other food van operators, maybe speaking to the bank about a loan.

He told me I was selfish and asked why I never thought he could succeed at anything.

I felt like laughing and saying, 'Because you never do! How many times have I backed you when you've said you'll try, and then been disappointed?

I can't keep doing it! I'm done.'

But instead I pressed my lips together and turned away, tears coming to my eyes at the unfairness of it all. Selfish!

Sam stood up and I could tell he was hugely angry.

With a groan of frustration he thrashed his arms around, as if he didn't know what to do with his body. Then he picked up the vase with the moth pupa, ran to the door and threw it as hard as he could onto the concrete floor of the porch, the vase exploding in every direction like a great, glass bomb. I screamed in shock, and the noise seemed to shake Sam out from the rage that had possessed him, and his face crumpled. Then he turned and ran out of the house, slamming the front door behind him.

I left it there all night, the shattered glass. When I went out in the morning to sweep it all up, I couldn't find the chrysalis anywhere. Had it been flung into the garden, still stuck to a piece of glass? Or had the chrysalis itself detached from the glass and got caught up in the leaves and dirt around the porch? Either way, I didn't think the pupa could possibly have survived.

But then I saw it, back under the table where I first found it, surrounded by shards. I reached out for it and found that it was no longer heavy and firm to the touch, but light and papery, with a split in the casing from one end to the other.

It had lived, apparently, and it had emerged.

So I've been waiting to see if the moth will turn up.

I don't even know what it will look like, but it'll be big, that's for sure. Unlike the common greyish ones that flutter around the porch light right now, it will be something more impressive, something unusual. If the cocoon is anything to go by, maybe it'll be chocolatey brown, rimmed with a subtle sheen of gold or mauve as moth wings often are, patterned with subtle artistry that will repay careful inspection.

I sit in the quiet and try not to look at the light, which hovers on the edge of my vision like a small, close moon.

The Bonfire

Kate Murdoch

The bitter stench of hot tarmac and the tang of seaweed filled my memories from that summer.

Sun-spilled days flowed one into the other. My brother Tim and I dragged our shins through the rank mud flats at the end of the beach, bubbles of air popped through the greyish-brown murk as we lifted our legs. Weeds were strewn over the surface and crabs scuttled out of the way.

I had heard Tim whispering with his new mates. Some of them were locals, others from the caravan park on the corner. They sniggered and I heard my name.

'What do you think of Skater?' Tim asked, his eyes hidden behind mirrored sunglasses. I was silent, thinking of the small, sleek-haired boy who spoke only in single words: *cool, ace, yep.*

I shrugged. 'He's okay, I guess.'

I was only ever interested in the tall, loping friends of my brother. The family friend, the one from his school with the beautiful eyebrows and penetrating stare. Boys my age were fumbling and awkward, distant from the ideas and fixations I inhabited. To talk with them, I had to try and think like them, to remove myself from the safety of my mind.

'He likes you,' muttered Tim, his leg caked in shimmering mud as he plunged forward.

I doubted it. I knew the group of misfits who formed my brother's summer gang were just idle and needing a focus. Placing me and the uncertain boy together was an experiment.

As coral streaked the sky, I followed my brother over to Greg's place, several streets away from our beach house. The group of boys and one girl lounged in haphazard formations in the fibro extension. Big Al waved us in as if he owned the place, his stomach straining against a moth-eaten t-shirt, black hair gelled at the sides. He was flanked by flame-haired Greg who aimed to please with self-conscious jokes. Simone was draped over a couch arm in a pink mini. She held herself as if she understood the power and purpose of her body.

On the beanbag was Skater, hands jammed into the pockets of his windcheater. He barely glanced up, his gaze on the TV. On the screen, a sumo wrestler was limbering up in a ring. Greg laughed his high chortle. 'I taped this. It comes on at 3 am on SBS. Check out the rolls.'

'You're an idiot,' sneered Big Al. 'Lauren, you can sit on the pouf.' Greg snorted and Skater's one eye stared, the other concealed beneath a swathe of pale hair.

The pouf was sticky under my thighs. I waited for the inevitable, wishing I'd refused. Big Al's voice was syrupy. 'How about you and Skater go into Greg's room and get to know each other?'

My heart thudded as I stood and resisted the urge to walk out. Skater flushed and followed me to the room, its light underwater green from Greg's drawn curtains. We sat as far away from each other on the twisted sheets as possible. Skater withdrew further behind his hair. I wondered why everyone assumed I was attracted to infants. My friends in Melbourne had set me up with a pink-skinned boy who smelled of soap, and now my brother with this mute offering.

'I hear you skate a lot,' I said, taking shallow breaths. The room was infused with sweat, unwashed bedding and a ripe, sour scent.

'Yes, I do.'

'You must love it.'

The conversation dwindled. I could almost hear his brain feverishly working to conjure words. I watched his mouth open and close a few times before rising to my feet and leaving the room.

We arrived home late, my parents sat at the empty kitchen table. Dad's face was blotched maroon.

'With those no-hopers again?' he asked.

'Now, Walter,' said Mum, her gaze on her clasped hands.

'Druggies the lot of them.'

Tim sighed. 'They're all right, Dad. You don't even know them.'

I had seen the way Mum pursed her lips when Big Al came over, greeting him with strained courtesy. Dad was more transparent, holding his newspaper up high, his words laced with contempt.

Dad stared Tim down. 'We're not coming again next summer. Thinking of selling up.'

My brother gaped. 'We've come here for ten years. It's a tradition.'

'Traditions can change.'

Tim stalked off to his bedroom.

I clutched the door handle in the back of an olive-green Falcon with no seatbelts, Simone shrieking with laughter next to me as we roared around corners. The driver was a friend of Greg's—he swung the wheel like he was playing a video game, his hands barely touching the plastic.

Tim was in Big Al's car ahead of us—we were on our way to a party at the back beach. Light skimmed the horizon, burnt orange meeting indigo as we approached the beach. My chest tightened and Simone grasped my arm, her fingernails sharp.

I had watched as she made up her face in Greg's bathroom, clipped on her purple bra, shrugged on an asymmetric t-shirt. Her limbs were burnished and lean, her hair permed and electric down her back.

Ahead, the dunes were monolithic, outlined against dark velveteen sky. The brakes squealed as the car swung and jolted to a stop.

A licking fire blazed on the sand as we emerged from the path. In the shadows around it, people crouched and leant their heads together, their bodies shifting in tandem with the flames. Simone held the crook of my arm as we edged closer. Laughter rang out, voices rose and fell. I sat on the chilled sand and heat embraced me, prickling my skin. Big Al muttered some introductions as he saw us, and Tim raised a stubby in my direction. Greg's face was alight, the shadows pooling beneath his cheekbones as he nudged the boy next to him.

'That's Simone,' he said with a smirk. 'She's up for it. This is Marcus.'

'Fuck off,' scowled Simone and slouched over, hugging her knees.

A couple of boys hooted with laughter and Greg glared, his red hair curled around his head like a funhouse clown.

I was relieved to have escaped attention, then felt a rush of guilt. Beer was passed to me and I gulped it—a sour taste as it fizzed in my mouth. The flames leapt gold, purple and brightest blue as wood snapped and collapsed. There was only the circle of light, low chatter, a ribbon of moonlight on the water as waves crashed in.

Simone leant her face to my ear. 'Greg never recovered from the time he asked me out and I blew him off. Plus, I never laugh at his jokes.'

'They're not funny,' I said and buried my bare feet in the sand.

Marcus sauntered over and sat next to Simone. He appraised her with hooded eyes, holding himself with confident languor. She turned toward him, like a flower opening to the sun, unwrapped her arms from her legs. Her voice warmed as he asked questions. From the other side of the fire, Skater watched me.

Lulled by the snaking flames and beer, I stretched out, cradled my head with my hand. Listening to the voices, roaring sea, crackling fire and my heartbeat, I let go.

When I woke there was a space where Simone had been. My limbs were stiff and the fire had ebbed—embers glowed beneath. Fewer people sat around me. I rose and found Tim on the other side.

'Have you seen Simone?' I asked, blood rushing in my ears.

'Not for a while,' he said. 'She went towards the dunes with Marcus.' He frowned. 'You need to stay here.'

I shook my head. 'I'm going to find her.'

Tim grumbled as I left, but didn't follow.

There was only one path into the dunes, near a rise in the sand. The moon illuminated the way as I trudged upwards. The wooden posts stood where I remembered them, surrounded by seagrass. In the distance, a faint cry sounded. My heart raced and I broke into a run.

At the bottom of the wall of sand was a flat area, cast in silver. The sand was a sea of its own, undulating with shadows, dotted with grasses. Marcus stood to one side, smoking a cigarette while Greg pinioned Simone to the ground, jeans at his knees. He groaned as his buttocks clenched and released. His hand clamped over her mouth as she lurched and twisted beneath him, strangulated sounds escaping from beneath his fingers. I stood immobile, still unseen. Nausea burned in my throat as I dug my nails into my palm and held my breath. I scanned the ground for a weapon, a stick, anything. There was nothing.

I felt a presence behind me and turned to see Skater, his mouth open. Our eyes locked in a moment of understanding and we nodded before charging forwards.

'Get off her!' I screamed and Skater bent to the ground, gathering sand. As Greg rolled off, Skater threw the fistfuls at his eyes and I joined him, my teeth bared. Greg sputtered and held up his arms against the deluge. Simone scrambled to her feet and yanked up her underpants, keening. I turned and saw Marcus sprint down the path, the orange end of his cigarette fell behind him.

Tim, Skater, Simone and I walked home. We held her up on either side, mascara streaked her cheeks, her t-shirt ripped. Her shoes scuffed the concrete as we propelled her forward. Aside from some mewling sounds, she was quiet.

My parents stood sentinel at the door. Dad called the police as Mum sat Simone in an armchair. Her story tumbled out between gasps, hands knotted and knuckles white. Marcus had tricked her, lured her to the dunes as a favour to Greg. I stroked her hair as she wept.

We drove past farmland, ocean beaches, vast opalescent skies, my brother and I sullen in the back, our bags shoved high on the seat between us. Tim had argued with our father before we left, promised to find new friends. I watched unseen from the hall as he evoked family memories: pistachio scoops at the ice-cream parlour, sailing past the rocks, the ferry to French Island.

I knew better—Dad was slow to make decisions, but immovable once he arrived at them.

I circled the garden, storing mental images of the hibiscus bush where we had plucked magenta blooms to thread behind our ears, the twisting crenulated trunks of the banksias near the gate, the rickety bench where I hid, my knees drawn up, to read.

As the car sped on the freeway, I thought how a series of hours could wreak irrevocable change—a girl's life imprinted with a story, a part of her stolen. Simone's spirit had sparked and ignited like the flames of the bonfire. I hoped she would rise and renew, that what made her so alive would help her transcend.

Dead Dreams

Sandeep Kumar Mishra

In his dreams, Rajan searches for the ghosts, tracing their footsteps in the dirt. He is back in his hometown—he knows these roads. The moonlight shivers on his skin. The crooked streets rattle around him. His heart burns in his chest. *Baba, Mama. Where are you?*

He runs, following the path laid out for him. The streets smell like smoke. Everything is hazy and deserted, shuttered up and locked away. He knows his neighbours behind each door, but no one steps out to help him. Rajan keeps running. *Please, if I could just see you one more time. I didn't know it would be the last time. I would have said so much more. Baba, Mama.*

When he looks up, the ghosts blur in the distance, like a poorly developed photo, but he can still sense the sadness etched upon their faces. Grief sweeps over Rajan like a monsoon. He drops to his knees. The ground begins to crumble. A dark pit opens underneath him—a grave, cloying and sticky with the scent of death. The spirits watch from a distance, cold in the low moonlight.

Rajan falls.

He wakes up with a jolt. It's still dark outside. Warm air filters in from the cracked window by his cot. The only sound in his cell is his own unsteady breath, and what sounds like the rustle of paper. He looks at his journals, but they lie still across the room, untouched. He looks out the window. Two beady black eyes stare back at him. The snake hisses, but it sounds more like a shriek of mocking laughter. He doesn't sleep for the rest of the night.

Dawn spills like pale pink soup over the horizon, bringing with it a searing heat that refuses to break. The prisoners queue up to receive sloppy rations of oatmeal ladled into their bowls.

Rajan sits down at a table. He's made it a point to write every day—it's the only thing keeping him sane. A flip of the journal's pages shows his journey: first, raw confusion; then, legal jargon for later lookup; lastly, feverish thoughts of revenge as he realises what has happened. After, a dull acceptance of his fate. Then a sudden jolt back to confusion as the pandemic hit and the world spun upside down.

He still feels an ache in the pit of his chest, a heartburn he can't get rid of. Rajan used to take pride in his sensitive emotions—it made him a better poet, after all, and his poetry landed him a teaching position at a prestigious university. Now, though, he wishes he could turn off his mind. There's too much to feel.

'Hey.' One of the other prisoners—a skull-inked man aptly nicknamed Bones—nudges Rajan's side. 'Stop writing, professor. What's the point? None of us are ever getting out of here.'

Rajan does not spare him a glance, and continues writing. 'The words are the point.' If he doesn't write, then the words haunt him in the dark, and he doesn't sleep.

Bones grunts. 'That's deep, man. I bet if I was that deep, my wife wouldn't've left me.'

Rajan has heard it all by now. If I hadn't met her…if he hadn't pissed me off so much…if the cops hadn't been nearby that day…Rajan has never played their game. There's no point in wondering about the past. He isn't even sure about enough details about his case to wish differently.

All Rajan knows is this: one minute, he was an esteemed professor travelling internationally to attend a literary seminar. The next, airport security found a bag of white powder in his carry-on, and there was a global pandemic. The world was having a collective panic attack, and his pleas of innocence were lost in the cries of a million others.

Mid-morning, he gets a migraine, which makes him scream and kick his cot in frustration. He's been plagued by headaches his whole life, but they got viciously worse when he came to Australia eight months ago.

Rajan curls up in a corner of the room, hands wrapped around his knees. White spots dance in his vision. It feels like a hammer is raining blows down on the back of his skull. When things got this bad, his wife used to soothe him with a cool compress. He passes out with her name on his tongue.

In his hazy, pain-filled sleep, he sees a snake. Mottled spots of green blot the snake's body like mould. The snake hisses at him. The desert blurs around him. The prison is at his back. He's outside. He's free, if he can just get past the snake in his path.

Rajan picks up a stick from the ground, intending to shoo the snake away. Before he can, the snake shrieks and flails, tail lashing on the ground. Rajan jumps back. The snake hurls itself towards him. Breathing hard, Rajan looks down at his wrist. Two pin-point pricks of fangbite are embedded in his skin. Poison seeps slowly through his veins. Dizziness overwhelms him, and he collapses. He wakes up smothered in sheets from head to toe, like a funeral shroud.

The rest of the week flits by like a ghost in the mist. Time blurs, and Rajan struggles to find things to record in his journal. He is starting to forget the details of his family's faces. He draws pictures of them in his journal. Does his father wear two rings or one? Does his mother have a mole under her right eye or left? It strikes Rajan with a deep, tolling sadness that he will never again be able to look at them.

With nothing else to do, Rajan starts recording his dreams. In this half-twilight, he writes:

October 18, 2020. The ghosts came to visit me again. This time, it was my children. They danced around me in a circle, chanting, 'Baba's dead! Baba's dead!'

I tried to tell them that I wasn't dead, that I was just away temporarily, but they couldn't hear or see me. I tried to embrace them, ruffle their hair, but I couldn't touch them. It was as if I were invisible or a ghost. Am I becoming a ghost? My feet are straight, and bhuta are restless, transient things. I am not ever-moving. I am stuck. I hate being so stuck.

October 19, 2020. Last night, I saw the snake—the same snake I always do. I killed the snake. But the snake returns. It bit itself—a perfect, pure, ouroboros. It behaves like it also wants to die. I don't know how to feel about this. The snake returns.

'What's up, dude?' Bones prods Rajan's shoulder. They're in the yard. 'You look even more depressed than usual, which is saying something.'

'Nothing. I'm fine.'

'Seriously, Professor, you're worrying me. Is it the nightmares? Are they getting worse?'

Rajan blinks. Water drips down his chin. 'How did you know?'

'You cry in your sleep.' At Rajan's expression, Bones rushes to reassure him. 'We all get the bad dreams, dude. We've all been through something heavy.'

Rajan says, 'I think...I might be cursed. I don't know.' He gestures to his chest. 'All my emotions are like water, filling me up, drowning me. There's only so much grief a person can take.'

Bones sits next to him. 'What do you see in the dreams?'

'A snake,' Rajan says, holding up his hands. 'About this big. We fight. I kill it. The snake returns.'

Bones scratches his head. 'The same dream? Every night?'

Rajan shrugs. 'Pretty much.'

'Cool,' says Bones. 'In my dreams, my wife always yells at me all the time.' Rajan laughs humorlessly. 'If you are having the same dream every night, a spirit is haunting you. You need to do something to appease it.'

'Like what?'

'Well, leave bowls of honey and milk outside for the fairies to eat. Maybe just do something different to help it out? Saying that aloud, it all sounds pretty nutty.'

Rajan gestures to the prison yard, to the barbed-wire walls and the world at large, where panic and a pandemic consume them all.

'If you ask me, anything's worth a try.'

Rajan takes no sleeping pills that night. He lies on his cot, arms folded over his chest, and watches the moonlight seep like spoiled milk through the window. He closes his eyes. Here he is again. The jail behind him, the snake in front of him. Imprisonment or death. Are those his only options?

The snake bares its fangs, which curve like crescent moons in the light. Rajan picks up the stick. The wood is familiar in his hands, grooved from his grip.

'Back off,' he tells the snake. It hisses at him. 'I mean it.'

The snake lunges for him. Rajan dodges away, swiping the stick out to protect his bare feet.

The snake writhes and coils. Its tail thumps in the dirt again. Rajan hits it with the stick. It howls.

This is his dilemma: he can wound the snake, but whenever he closes in for the killing blow, it finds a way to bite him. Slaughtering it only results in both of them dying.

Do something different. Break the cycle. Bones' voice whispers in the back of Rajan's head.

Rajan backs away. The snake follows.

'Stop,' Rajan says. 'I don't want to hurt you.' The snake's black eyes fix on the weapon in his hand. So Rajan sets the stick down.

The snake rises up, twists its head to consider him. Its eyes reflect the white-chip light of the stars above.

'Go,' Rajan says. 'You're released. You don't have to die to be free.'

The snake places its body back on the flat ground. Then it slithers off into the desert. Rajan takes a step forward into the night. Nothing stops him. For once, there are no ghosts, no migraines, no spirit-snakes waiting to strike. He is free.

The next morning, a guard comes to visit his cell, rapping loudly on the bars.

'Hey. Wake up.'

Rajan hasn't slept. This time, it wasn't insomnia, but indecision: he is burdened by his choice to let the snake go free. What has he set loose? The nightmare has so warped his life that he can't help but imagine it will impact the waking world, too. For all his metaphors, for all his knowledge of spirits and curses and dreamscapes, he doesn't know what he's done.

'Get going,' the guard snaps. 'You're leaving.'

Rajan blinks. Sits up. 'Leaving?'

'In three hours.'

He almost doesn't want to ask. It's too much to hope for. 'Where— where am I going?'

'I don't know. Back to wherever you came from, I guess,' the guard sneers, but Rajan barely registers the jab. He's going to get out.

He glances down at the page in his journal, where he has written the first scrawling lines of a poem:

Today I did not kill the snake
I set it free
It will return to the wild
I will wait for its mercy
And it will return to me.

He asks, though he already suspects the answer: 'Why?'

'Prison's full—we need more space than usual because of the pandemic.

You're a minor offender. Your sentence was shortened.' The guard tosses a piece of paper at him, presumably some sort of official court document. 'Pack your stuff.'

Three hours later, he's out the door.

Rajan breathes in the sweet desert air. The heat doesn't bother him, and his migraine has faded. Clouds of dust bloom like flowers. The world is still. Even the tumbleweed has stopped its travels to watch him.

As he takes his first steps as a free man, a snakeskin snaps beneath his shoe.

The Birdwatcher

Christine Johnson

It was the night before the funeral. In Doug's dream, Valerie approached. She strode over desert, pavement and vast grass plains to arrive in the station yard. Doug stood at the homestead's window, waiting, watching.

Valerie wore a flowing ivory garment. A thick leather gauntlet covered her lower left arm. She held the arm up, elbow crooked at an angle. Perched upon her wrist was a magnificent Wedge-tailed Eagle.

Doug marvelled at its muscular build and stark stare, set behind a hooked beak. One metre from proud head to tail-tip, with powerful legs and sharp talons, he thought it the mightiest bird he'd ever seen. Valerie stroked the bronze feathers on the bird's chest, before smoothing her fingers along its splendid wings. The telescopic-eyed hunter bowed its head, submitting to her caress. As she straightened her arm, the bird responded to her signal, taking flight. Grand, slow wing beats curved it up and away.

Doug opened the door. Valerie stepped inside. A fire burned in the kitchen stove. Embraced by its warmth, Doug sensed another closed door behind him. It hid a rank gloom and his shrivelled mother, putrid hair spreading like a stain.

He woke, sweating, blood beating in his temples.

Rain thumped on the roof. He calmed his rapid breathing, concentrating on vital moisture slurping into parched earth surrounding the homestead. Such a noise should delight, but the bizarre dream clung to his mind. Air was chill in the boyhood room, which had become his adult room. He rose, wearing yesterday's shirt, gathered his jeans from where they'd fallen the night before, and pulled them over his legs.

His mother's absence met him. Without need, he crept past her door, avoiding creaking boards Time had become his once her terminal illness took over. Despite essential work around the station, he'd spent long

87

stretches in the kitchen, drinking tea. Freed at last to imagine what his life might have been.

This morning he stood outside by the gate, fine rain rinsing his face. He savoured the rare scent of wet earth. After a long, dry summer, he heard the thirsty land alongside him, guzzling.

Jean, his sister, had telephoned the day before, her chatter tense.

'Valerie's in town,' she said at last. 'Ran into her at the supermarket.'

'Right.'

It relieved Doug. His first thought hearing her anxiety: *thank Christ, she doesn't want to sell the station.* But then he registered what she'd said.

'I…asked her to come. Sorry, didn't know what to do. Doug, you there?'

He'd hung up, Jean still talking.

He opened the gate. A few steps into the paddock, he looked up. Far away, he caught sight of an eagle rising on a thermal, soaring in ever-widening circles. To clear raindrops from his eyes, he closed and then opened them. The eagle had gone.

He almost didn't recognise her. She came late, slipping in while the priest was talking. Doug turned to see a stylish woman in her fifties with a smooth shell of streaked hair. Then he spotted the way her head cocked to one side, like a curious Striated Grasswren. He spun back, staring ahead, hands clammy in his lap.

Jean stepped up next, gripping the lectern. She spoke about the difficult hand life dealt their mother, left with two children and the station when their father walked away. How, despite that, she always had the guts to make tough choices.

'Hell,' said Jean. 'Reckon Mum had more balls than most men.'

Everyone laughed. 'It was hard living with Dad. Big-noting bastard he could be.' Knowing murmurs ran through the older women. 'Still, you'll remember Mum dancing, her fondness for a beer. Took pleasure where she could.'

Doug stared at the closed casket, thinking of the corpse within. Jean's words conjured how, as a boy, his mother's body awed him: the way it could chop wood, dowse a cow, spin a graceful turn around the lounge-room to the radio's sound.

After his father left, she taught Doug to dance. A tall, solid boy, he was a good size match for her even at age twelve. Her warm, beer-scented breath caressed his cheek.

'That's my lad. You're handsome. Like your father, only nice.' He enjoyed it, at first. The praise, the swaying, holding his mother's body in his arms.

It compensated for the way his father embarrassed him, called him weak. Ridiculed him for his interest in things like native birds.

'And of course,' Jean was saying, 'we mustn't forget Doug. Pulled out of school to help Mum when I married, when he was only fifteen. And caring for her after she got sick, working, keeping things running. I know what it cost him. Not all, but some. So, Doug, I want to say thank you.'

Jean looked at him. There were tears in her eyes—and something else. It made the space spin and his breath catch in his chest. Tight-lipped, he concentrated on the thought of the wasted body in the coffin. Hands on a hollow chest, bones inside twisted fingers. How, once buried, those thin bones would be what the worms would first nibble clean.

Sunlight fell through the chapel's windows. Doug looked at his own hands, knotted for Jean's speech. He unclenched his fingers and spread them. Imagined them as flight feathers ending an impressive wingspan, carrying him to dizzying altitudes.

He was standing at the back of the hall by the open door, nursing a beer and enjoying the sky's fresh-washed blue, when behind him he sensed a presence. He breathed in, unable to move.

When he turned, she was there. Valerie. His mouth went dry.

'Hello Doug.'

'Valerie.'

He fell silent. They stood side by side, awkward after all these years, watching people mill about. Doug glanced at her. So close.

'A drink?'

'No.'

She looked on the verge of tears. When she shook her head, her hair caught the light. His stomach lurched. If he could reach out, take a strand between his fingers.

'Oh, Doug,' she said, voice breaking as if she read his thoughts.

After that, things seemed easier. The old intimacy crept back. She talked about her marriage, how it ended. How she'd recovered, taken up teaching again. He told her about working the station, improvements he'd made since taking over from his mother. His plans, now that she was dead.

'And do you still study birds? Keep that journal of different species you find?'

'Not really.'

Then he contradicted himself, describing his last expedition. A remote place, the smell of dirt, the sun's heat. His watching came with dreaminess, a stillness like no other. That was when he knew contentment. Those times, he thought, that's when I think of you.

She smiled. 'You always were one for the birds, Doug.' Encouraged, he told her about the old cottage. How he'd cared for it over the years, how the citrus trees she'd planted were mature, what good fruit they gave.

'There's oranges on the trees now,' he said. 'Why not come taste them?'

'I'm not sure.'

'Come on.'

He held her gaze until she nodded.

'Look at us,' she conceded. 'Two old fools.' But Doug didn't feel like an old fool. He felt great, almost heroic.

Valerie agreed to come the following Saturday, a week after the funeral. Doug pushed her to come sooner, but she replied he should thank her for coming at all, given everything that had happened. She laughed, saying it, but he felt the sting in her words.

He rose early the morning after the funeral, his heart light. The sun shone as, whistling, he walked to the cottage. At the cottage, he halted. Despite his words to Valerie, the garden was overrun, trees surrounded by fallen, rotted fruit. Inside, faded paint peeled from the walls. Within the woodstove, he found a rat's nest. 'Shit!' This place was to have been his and Valerie's. He spent the next days working hard.

Up with the sun and not stopping until dusk, he pruned the fruit trees, repainted walls and poisoned the rats.

One evening traipsing home, muscles aching, he tilted his head and noticed an imposing structure built of sticks in the neighbourhood's tallest tree. Its position commanded an impressive view. A nest for a pair of eagles, Doug was sure of it! These were monogamous birds, mating for life. Soon there would be two adult birds defending their territory, hunting, laying eggs and rearing chicks. If food was scarce, the largest chick might even kill and eat its siblings. Nature wasn't sentimental with survival.

At the cottage the next morning, the door creaked open behind him. It was Jean.

'What you doing?'

'Stuff. Might move in.'

'That right?' She looked around. 'Could be nice, peaceful.'

Her eyes sought more from him, but he kept on scrubbing.

'Well, can you help me clean out Mum's room at the house? Reckon it's time.'

They started with the bed. It smelt of piss and illness. They burned the mattress in the yard. Doug watched the smoke furl into the sky. Clothes filled garbage bags that Jean tossed in her station wagon to drop off at Vinnie's. They disinfected the floor and walls. Jean cleared the dressing-table and held up two photos.

'Their wedding day,' she winced, describing the first.

The other was their mother, young, in a floral dress. She looked pretty, innocent. Doug took the photo, stared at it, and handed it back.

'You keep them,' he said.

Everything finished, he waited to see Jean off. She hesitated.

'This place is yours now, Doug. You're free.'

Eyes on the smouldering fire remains in the yard, Doug thought of Valerie's visit the next day.

'Yes,' he said, 'maybe I am.'

That night, he dreamed his mother came into his bedroom. The mother of his teens, her skin glowing in the moonlight. She sat on his bed, smoothing his hair. Murmured he was a good boy, clever and handsome. Then, while one hand kept smoothing his hair, her other hand moved below the covers, eased its way down and began the fondling movements he'd learned to dread. He screamed. But it was the silent scream that comes with sleep.

He woke with a headache. Rose, shaved, showered, and dressed as the dream sat in his stomach like a lump of lead.

He arrived at the cottage, planning to make tea and serve it to Valerie. Then they'd pick oranges.

He stood in front of the stove, the black iron gleaming. Paper and kindling stuffed in, he let the match die in his hand. Hunched on the floor, he stared at the matchbox. The drone of Valerie's car came down the track. It whined as the engine struggled up the hill.

He imagined Valerie entering, taking her in his arms, feeling her body beneath her clothes. Then he remembered the look on her face all those years ago. The morning of their wedding when he'd turned up. Told her he couldn't go through with it. The way her Grasswren-cocked head straightened as she listened. Only this time, he saw her pupils growing larger, taking on the glare of an eagle. One that would kill.

A knock at the cottage door. He didn't move. 'Doug?' He didn't answer. Shrank into shadow beside the stove. 'Hello?'

He heard her check the house. Search the garden, calling his name. Crawled forward and peered through the window as she stopped by the citrus trees. Saw her reach up and touch the bright fruit before standing, head down. For a long moment, she waited. Then she returned to her car, and left.

When the last dust settled, Doug stepped outside. Numb, he walked back to the main house. Tried to plan spring: the calves, the crops. He reached the large nest seen earlier and gazed upwards. Unoccupied. Not an eagle in sight.

At the homestead, he put on the kettle. Its ordinary thrumming was comforting.

'Bird watching,' he said, 'out bush, tomorrow.'

Homecoming

James Noonan

My father was laid to rest on a cold drizzly morning in late April. I didn't remember much of the service—I was jetlagged and my thoughts were still on Stephen, and how we'd left things in New York. He'd wanted to come with me, but I told him it wasn't worth the cost, that I'd only be flying in and out. It had turned into an argument that lasted half the night.

There were only a dozen or so mourners at the church, and fewer still made it to the cemetery. I stood with my sister beneath a black umbrella as strangers came forward and offered their condolences, tossed flowers into the open earth. Most of them, I realised, were football players from my father's era, now barely recognisable—their faces lined and ruddy, bellies spilling out of their shirt fronts. My sister did most of the talking. I supposed they mistook my silence for grief.

Anna invited the men back to her place for afternoon tea. They looked ill at ease in her living room, hunched over finger sandwiches and tartes tatin. While Anna was in the kitchen, I did the obligatory rounds and thanked them for coming. They asked me about the usual things—work and whether I thought Trump stood a chance—before the conversation dried up. A few of them remarked on my resemblance to my father, and even shared an anecdote about his younger days. I smiled and pretended I knew what they were talking about. Anna came in and put the footy on—Carlton were playing—and the men gathered around the television, eager as children.

Anna's husband, Matthew, called in then with the kids and said a quick hello before leaving for work. He'd taken them to the park while we were out. Somehow Mikayla remembered me and darted over to give me a hug. I felt a sudden stab of guilt that I hadn't brought her anything, a snow globe or similar souvenir from the city—wasn't that what visitors were supposed to do with young children? She didn't seem bothered; she was intent only on showing me her room.

'Later, honey,' Anna said as she sunk into a stool at the kitchen table and poured us both a glass of wine. Mikayla ran up the stairs feigning a tantrum. I smiled at Anna and shifted Tommy in my lap. This was the first time I was meeting my nephew. I wasn't sure exactly how old he was. He was warm and heavy in my arms and kept staring up at me, gently stroking my stubble.

'Is he sleeping through the night?' I asked, struggling for the right question.

'Sort of,' Anna said, between sips. 'I'm up with him usually once or twice.' I studied my sister while she filled me in on everything I'd missed out on. She'd lost a lot of weight since I'd seen her last—three years ago or so, right before I left for New York. Her face was pallid and drawn and her ash blonde hair had thinned out. I wondered whether it was the stress of the last few months with our father, or if this was how she looked now.

'He was good with them, you know,' Anna was saying, topping up her glass. 'You should have seen him with Mikayla—playing around on the floor for hours. And I can't tell you how many times she made him watch *Frozen* and *Finding Nemo* and all the rest. She adored him. She doesn't really get it—you know, where he's gone. She keeps asking where Pop is. I've tried to explain, but it's hard—they don't have any notion of time or absence yet.'

I didn't know what to say so I just lifted my glass. I was grateful, then, for the sound of the doorbell.

Anna returned with a small grey-haired woman named Julie, who had come bearing flowers and a fruit basket. She worked for Meals on Wheels and had delivered food to my father for the last two years, ever since his first stroke. She couldn't stay—she was midway through a shift—but she'd wanted to call around and pay her respects. Her raspy voice broke a little when she hugged me.

'You're the boy. In America.'

I said that I was, wondering what he'd told her.

'Good Lord, you're the spitting image of him.'

I excused myself, saying it was nice to meet her, and took a fresh tray of beers in for the guys. They were muttering at the telly, gesturing in frustration. I checked the score; Carlton were down by four goals. I noticed the players were all wearing black arm bands, presumably for my father. None of them had probably even been born when he was at the club.

Silently, I ducked out the side door and withdrew my vape. I'd been dying for a smoke all day. The rain had stopped; there was now only the soft steady drip from the gutters and the leaves. The trees lining the road were ablaze in colour—burnt reds and rich golden yellows. The faint smell of woodsmoke was in the air. I felt a pang of nostalgia that I couldn't quite place.

'God, I knew you'd be the vaping type.'

Anna came out in a cardigan, lighting her own cigarette.

'You should try it,' I said. 'It's better for your health.'

'I've quit, anyway,' she shrugged.

'And doing a sterling job of it.'

She exhaled in my face. 'I just didn't want you feeling lonely out here.'

A silence settled between us, not the first of the day. I pulled out my phone and checked the time. I had to be at the airport in an hour.

'Hey, I read that book of yours,' Anna said.

'By the young Indian writer?'

'Oh my God, I cried my eyes out. I mean, a lot of it went over my head, you know me. But it was heart breaking. Poor Matthew kept asking what was wrong, I'd be sat up in bed each night blubbering like a baby.'

I smiled and shivered against the chill breeze. 'Sorry.'

'What's he like in person?'

'Lovely. A dream to work with—so humble. And, for a short story collection, it completely overshot our expectations. It just made the shortlist for one of the major prizes, which is unheard of for a debut.'

'My brother,' Anna said, looking out onto the leafy street. 'The famous young editor.'

'Hardly,' I countered, lifting the vape to my lips. 'That was my first ever acquisition. I'm still just a lowly assistant.'

A collective cheer erupted from inside the house. One of the guys seemed to be shouting my father's name.

'Whatever happened,' I said, 'to what's-her-name—the woman he was seeing for a while?'

'*Karen*? Oh God, they split ages ago. Even before you left. Was only a matter of time, I suppose. She sent a really beautiful card. Said that funerals weren't really her thing.'

95

Another silence fell. I shifted uncomfortably on my feet. I sensed what was coming next.

'Are you seeing anyone?' my sister asked, her voice slightly changed, eyes following a passing car. I hadn't told her about Stephen, not once in two years. It felt cruel to, now.

'Not really. Nothing serious.'

She looked down at the ground and I could tell she wanted to say something else. I cut in to deflect her.

'Is there anything you need me to do while I'm here?'

She took a final drag and stubbed out the cigarette with her shoe. 'Nah. I mean, it would've been great if you could stay a bit longer. I'm meeting with his solicitor this week. I can ring you though with the details. Everything will be split fifty-fifty.'

'Everything?' I said, unable to help myself. 'His second-hand furniture and old trophies?'

She ignored the barb. 'He had some money put away. I don't know exactly how much, but half of whatever's there is yours.'

I pocketed my vape. 'I don't want it.'

'Well, tough. It's not my decision to make.'

'Just take it. Use it on the kids.'

'That's real big of you, Luke,' she said testily. 'What do you think that's gonna prove? That you'll have the last laugh?'

'I'm not trying to be difficult—'

'Look, it's coming to you whether you like it or not. Choose a fucking charity you want to donate to if you're so high and mighty. I know you're still living in that shoebox of an apartment so don't try and act like you can do without the money.'

I looked away, peeved that we were bickering before I had to leave, but also that she was right.

Dark blue clouds had swept in overhead. Anna came over and wrapped her arm around me. Her eyes were wet. 'I mean it, I really wish you could stay longer. If only to get some rest. You look like shit.'

I smiled, feeling the sting of tears myself. 'I've missed you too.'

There was another burst of applause from inside, louder and longer than before. It sounded like they'd won.

I sat in the airport bar, answering emails. Rain slid down the windows and the sky lit up intermittently. My flight was delayed. A waiter came over and I ordered another scotch.

I considered calling Stephen, but it was after two in the morning over there. Besides, I didn't know what to say, whether he even wanted to hear from me.

Suddenly I recalled the morning, a few months back, when my phone had started ringing in the dark and I answered without looking at the caller. There was a delay with the connection, but then I heard my father's voice. He sounded drunk, his words barely intelligible. He mentioned he'd seen a news alert of a snowstorm bearing down on the city. He was so matter of fact that I wasn't sure if he was initiating a topic for discussion or whether he was actually concerned for me. I told him I hadn't heard of any such storm. I was tired and irritable that morning, I couldn't remember exactly what I said, only that I'd been short with him. It was the last time we spoke.

I pulled up Stephen's number and sent him a short message, saying I was sorry and that I missed him. He wrote back within minutes—I supposed he was out with friends—telling me he'd be at JFK when I got in, that he couldn't wait to see my stupid face.

I tried to concentrate on the stack of pages before me; I'd brought several manuscripts over, figuring I could get some work done on the plane. But the words weren't sinking in, they may as well have been written in another language. I looked up at the telly above the bar and saw that they were recapping today's Carlton game. Then all of a sudden my father was on screen. They were showing his famous clashes with the umpires, including the spray that got him sent off in the '93 Grand Final and cost Carlton the flag. I did the calculation in my head and worked out that he was my age back then. Apart from the mullet and the muscles, I supposed we did look alike.

They cut to a panel of commentators who were sharing their memories of him. I couldn't hear what they were saying and I had the sudden urge to ask the bartender to turn the volume up. But then the moment passed. An announcement came on over the loudspeaker. My flight was being called.

Down into the Hellhole

Jim Brigginshaw

The boy watched his dad pound the carbide rocks with an iron bar. The foul-smelling powder he was making was fuel for his pit lamp. The naked hissing flame of that tiny brass lamp would be his only light in the pitch blackness of the coal mine.

As Tommy watched he wondered what it would be like beneath the earth. Going down into the dark world would be a real adventure. He'd asked his father many times to take him but the answer was always the same: 'Keep out of the pit. Look what it's done to me, coughing my guts out.'

The mine was killing Joe Anderson—a slow death from the disease miners called black lung. Years of breathing coal dust in the primitive hellholes that were the Queensland mines of the 1930s had left him fighting for breath, his body wracked by fits of coughing that seemed to be trying to tear his body apart.

The cough hit him now. The iron bar he was using fell from his hands and he held onto a post for support as the familiar gurgling in his chest erupted into a sneezing, coughing convulsion that left him gasping for air.

The boy waited until his dad had resumed pounding the carbide before asking once again to be taken down below.

The response was what he expected: 'I'd be mad to take a twelve-year-old kid into the dangers down the pit.'

Tommy pouted his disappointment. 'Then you won't take me, Dad?'

'I worry that some day, when you're looking for a job, you'll take one down below and finish up like me, coughing your way into a coffin.' Then he said something the boy thought he'd never hear: 'Maybe it *is* time for you to learn what it's like down there. It might convince you to never work under the ground.'

Tommy couldn't believe it. 'You mean you'll take me?'

'I'll take you, but only to make sure you'll never do it for a living.' Joe Anderson gave a bitter laugh. 'A living? It's more a killing than a living.'

Tommy was out of bed well before four—the train out to the mines went at four-thirty. He put on old clothes and went into the kitchen where his mother was cutting thick jam sandwiches that she put in an airtight billycan to keep out the taste of the mine. Next, she filled another can with sweet black tea that was steaming hot now but would be stone cold when it was the only liquid they had to drink down below.

It was only a short walk to the railway station and they didn't have long to wait for the train. The carriage was full of miners who kept up a happy banter until they reached the mine. Tommy had often pictured the scene. The tall tower was the poppet-head. Its rotating wheels dropped the miners down the shaft in a flimsy box they called the cage. He was looking forward to going down in the cage—it would be the highlight of his adventure.

The miners, when they left the train, congregated at the pit-top, impatient at the delay until deputies checked the mine for gases with a safety lamp and a canary. The all-clear, when it came, started a rush for the cage.

Tommy's dad avoided the cage and led him towards the gaping black mouth of a tunnel.

'We're not going down in the cage, Dad?'

'I am, you're not,' his father said. 'I've seen it scare people out of their wits. You'll go down the tunnel in a skip with one of the wheelers.'

The boy swallowed his disappointment.

At the tunnel mouth, a fit-looking young man waited, holding the reins of a shaggy pony. Hitched behind was a line of four small wooden wagons.

Joe Anderson introduced the wheeler as Snow. 'He'll take you down below and show you what goes on. Later on, he'll bring you around to where I work.'

He took the carbide lamp off the old cloth cap his son was wearing, pricked the burner with a piece of fine wire, struck a wax match and touched it to the lamp. It burst into a hissing white flame.

'Right, you're ready to go,' Joe Anderson said, fixing the lamp to the front of his son's cap. Tommy heard the naked flame spluttering and tried not to think of explosive underground gases.

He climbed into the black coal dust in the bottom of one of the wooden wagons. Snow clucked his tongue, the pit pony bent its back and moved into the tunnel mouth.

Darkness, more intense than the blackest of nights, closed in. They started down a steep incline, the flames from their carbide lamps creating dancing silhouettes on the tunnel walls. Above the boy's head, so close he could touch it, was the craggy roof with moss-lined cracks that seeped dark water. In front of the skip, twin wooden rails ran into the black abyss. On each side a row of rough timber props, so thin it seemed impossible they could hold up the masses of earth above them, stretched out like a line of leafless trees in a forest in hell. The thick hot air of the pit had the smell of vegetation that had rotted in stagnant water at the bottom of a well.

Further underground, the tunnel floor became steeper. The pit pony slithered as it struggled to hold back the skips. Rats, the size of half-grown cats, scurried out of the way.

The rumble of skip wheels on the wooden tracks, the grunting of the sliding pony as it held back its load, were the only sounds in the eerie surroundings. Apart from that, the tunnel was as quiet as the grave. Tommy tried not to think of graves.

The quiet changed at the pit bottom—there it was as busy and noisy as a city street. Bells clanged to start and stop the haulage winch. Clippers cursed as they coupled coal-laden skips to the haulage rope to be sent to the surface. Wheelers bustled about with their ponies, blackened bare-bodied men hurried everywhere.

Snow's pony hauled the empty skips into a series of black caves the miners called rooms. In each room, two miners, stripped to the waist, worked at the coalface swinging picks to bring down the coal to be shovelled into the skips. Their bodies were streaked with white tracks left by sweat as it coursed down the layer of coal dust that covered them. The men didn't stop working to talk; they were paid by the amount of coal they filled.

Snow left them empty skips and hauled away those they had loaded with glistening black coal. These were taken to be clipped to the haulage winch and sent to the pit-head.

In the next few hours, Snow took Tommy to places close to purgatory. Miners worked squatting on their haunches or bent double because the roof was too low to let them stand upright. Pieces of brattice, the hessian that was supposed to direct air flow, hung as limp and useless as wet washing on a clothesline. Any breath of stale hot air that managed to arrive swirled with choking black coal dust. In heat like a blast furnace, some men worked naked, standing in inky water up to their knees.

At home once, when his father was in a rare expansive mood, he'd told Tommy of a coal seam he'd worked in that was only twenty two inches high—a slot they'd cut into the coalface. He'd crawl into this and push coal out with his feet. His mate couldn't go into the tomb-like space—he'd been claustrophobic since childhood and daily had to force himself to go down into the dark confines of the mine.

When Snow took Tommy into the room where his dad and his mate worked stripped to the waist, the boy was pleased to see the seam was six or seven feet high and that at least it was dry. Dust swirled around the two men and his father coughed constantly, the hacking body-wracking convulsions the boy knew so well.

His father stopped shovelling to gasp, 'Well, what do you think of coal mining?'

Tommy shuddered. 'I never imagined it'd be like this.'

'Remember it so you'll never come down here to work.'

At crib break, they ate their sandwiches and drank their cold black sweet tea sitting on chunks of stone, watched by eyes that flashed red in the light of the carbide lamps. The smell of food had the big black pit rats congregating around their feet like dogs begging for scraps. Joe tossed them a crust and they fought over it, setting up a hideous squealing.

He said the miners fed the rats to keep them around. 'If we don't see any rats, it's time to get out. Rats know when disaster's about to happen—it's not only sinking ships they desert.'

Back on the job, Joe bored deep holes in the seam with a cumbersome hand drill, then took from a squat can shiny brass detonators, green fuse and plugs of gelignite wrapped in greasy paper. He gently tamped the explosives into the holes, then lit the fuse with his carbide lamp and yelled the mandatory warning: 'Fire!'

They took refuge behind pillars of coal. The explosions, when they came, were a series of muffled thumps. Tommy had expected much louder.

It was only mid-afternoon when they knocked off. It seemed early to stop work until Tommy remembered they'd been on the go since four in the morning.

He was surprised when they used the cage to return to the surface. His dad said that going up the shaft was nowhere near as scary as coming down.

The breathtaking upwards surge made the boy pleased he'd gone underground in the wheeler's skip. The shaft's rough walls, as they whizzed by, were wet and slimy backdrops lit by the flickering lamps.

He wasn't sorry when the cage reached the pithead and he was able to step out of it and take a deep breath. For the first time that day the air he breathed was cool and clean, not stifling, black with coal dust and smelling like rotting vegetation. He'd never noticed before how good fresh air was.

On the miners' train home, Tommy wore the grime of the day—mines had no washing facilities. He was covered in coal dust, only the whites of his eyes showed. It was the source of amusement for the miners in the carriage. 'The bosses will charge you for all that coal your boy's taking home,' one joked to his father.

Tommy didn't mind them making fun of him. He'd joined these hardy men in their dangerous job. He was dead tired but he'd never felt so close to his sick father. Now he knew what his dad had long endured to provide for his family.

'What did you think of the mine?' his father asked as they walked home down the hill.

'It was fun, Dad.'

'*Fun!?*' Joe Anderson was suddenly angry. 'You think today was *fun*? Hasn't it taught you *anything*? Look what that rotten mine's done to me. I'll tell you something, boy, you'll never work down below. If you do, it'll be over my dead body.'

He didn't have to convince his son that down the pit was no job for anyone. After what Tommy had seen that day, it was at the bottom of the list of what he wanted to do in life. He had a crazy idea he wanted to be a doctor.

But he was a coalminer's son. Only the rich could afford universities.

And the world was falling apart with the economic disaster called the Great Depression.

What he wanted was just a dream.

An impossible dream.

Eleven-Thirty
Sally Jane Smith

I lost my race with Carly.

To be fair, she had a head start. She'd already flown from Hanoi to Cape Town. I still had to travel from one continent to another, and back again.

By half past eleven. My unspoken promise was a news ticker scrolling on repeat. *By eleven-thirty.*

She could rest, while I dragged myself from a comfortless bed before daybreak, winged my way the seven hundred miles west to Istanbul and navigated the strait to the Asian shore. All she had to do was get to the neighbourhood church for one last farewell before she burrowed into the earth.

Would she be walked up the aisle on her father's arm, like a bride?

I don't know. I'll never ask.

Clipping myself into my seat, I wondered how she'd travelled. *Cradled in the lap of her brother, or mine? Stowed safely in an overhead compartment before they fastened their seatbelts? Maybe she was wedged between suitcases in the frigid hold.*

I don't know. Perhaps I'll ask, one day.

There was no escaping it: I'd let everyone down. But I'd get to my hotel room. Shut the door. Curl around the pillow I'd clutched–for solace–all the way from Australia. I'd do that for her.

By eleven-thirty.

It had all come together three weeks earlier: the dark before a Vietnamese dawn, the tired driver turning into the construction site, the forklift's prongs inching across a dimly lit road at head height. The motor scooter rebounding, skittering over the tarmac...

In a microsecond, it all broke apart.

There'd been two hours of barren existence. For her. He was already gone.

In all the most important ways, so was she. But still they fought a doomed battle to save her. Her shaved scalp—so vulnerable, so cold—would be evidence of that futile fight.

Such bitter irony when she, a paramedic, had rescued so many others.

Then the snarled knots of bureaucracy, unravelling at last to side-by-side coffins, a final slide into the flames of the crematorium.

Carly and Marck.

They'd wanted to spend the rest of their lives together. And they did.

The midnight glimmer of my phone was a betrayal, a treacherous line of characters spelling out the sentence of my niece's death.

In the hours that followed, I could have flown anywhere. To Vietnam, where the bodies lay waiting in icy limbo. To South Africa, where my family lay crumpled. Instead, I fled. I turned away from my lover's helpless face—his pain for me more than I could bear—measured the commute to Sydney's airport in ragged breaths, handed over my boarding pass for the flight I'd booked months before.

It was a surreal journey into the heart of Turkey, following the itinerary I'd plotted like the book I longed to write. Seven weeks of hotel confirmations, checklists, and ferry tickets hauled me through a fathomless swamp of grief, one interminable night to the next.

Istanbul's Ramadan drums roused me hours before sunrise on the day they flew from Cape Town to Hanoi to bring her home: Carly's brother, uncle, and the friend she'd lived with like a sister. They were in the air when I boarded a bus to Safranbolu and its Silk Road town of timber-built mansions. They'd walked the footsteps of her life, and its ending, by the time a dark doorway drew me into the centuries-old Cinci Hammam. There, a stranger in a sturdy black bikini bathed me like a baby, her stretch marks a medal of maternity, her pendulous breasts brushing my face as she cupped one hand over my eyes and rinsed my hair with the other.

In the bathhouse's dank chambers, she smelled of motherhood. She lathered and sluiced with the business-like efficiency of a cat pinning her kitten under one paw to scour every inch with a rough tongue.

After a scrubbing that would leave its mark in bruises, a sponge feathered across my skin. I lay face-down in a cloud of froth, the marble slab's warmth soaking into my bones and heating the sodden cotton *peştemal* that puddled beneath me. And a sudden anguish ripped me open. Silent wails spilled from my soul, my lips moving in the soapy liquid. *Carly's dead, Mommy. Carly's dead.*

In those moments I was a child again, my head in my mother's lap. My grief raged with an infant's wretched fury, the soundless syllables surging in an unstoppable torrent. *Mommy, Carly's dead.*

Until, just once, new words rang clear:

Ssshhh, it's okay. Mommy knows now.

Two faraway young bodies crumbled to ash while I lay in that city of saffron, my phone in my hand, in an airy room lined with Ottoman divans. Rain dripped from dancing leaves outside the wooden sash windows as a message from Hanoi flashed up on the screen: *It is done.*

The rows of a spreadsheet—each exotic location trapped in its cell—pulled me onward, but I was a distant spectator of my own body's pursuits. In Cappadocia's uncanny landscape, my arms and legs were a jumble clambering into the basket of a hot air balloon. In Sivas, my fingers sought relief in the sun-drenched bricks of a leaning minaret. On Mount Nemrut's snow-brushed road, my stomach twisted with every slip of the tires rolling up to the burial mound at the summit, its stone effigies holding silent vigil through the ages.

All this time, there was a chance for me to change course, to turn towards home. But how could I breathe in a church filled with people who believed she was gone?

Of course, I knew it was true. I wasn't a fool. But I didn't *believe* it. It made no sense! How could she be gone, when I could still feel that long-ago little girl, all elbows and knees, her angles softening into my curves, her burnished curls tucked under my chin as I turned the pages of that day's story?

The morning came when my brother would bury his daughter's ashes. *Wear bright colours to the funeral*, the message echoed through Facebook from post to post. *Take your shoes off for Carly, who trod the earth barefoot, wherever she could.*

I was up before the sun, piling pain into my suitcase. I'd skirted the edge of Turkey's east, but now I'd fly to Europe, to a glossy new airport that was the pride of Istanbul, then make my way to my bed on the Asian side of the world's only transcontinental capital city.

By eleven-thirty.

My baggage was already circling the belt when I arrived, but the shuttle bus idled for an eternity, precious minutes dissolving in the deep thrum of its engine. By the time it dropped me near the mouth of the Golden Horn, it was too late for the gentle ferry I'd hoped would carry me across the Bosporus. I'd have to descend into the concrete underground instead. But even as the train thundered through its underwater tunnel, I realised I wouldn't make it to the hotel.

As I hurried up the metro's steep steps and into the grey light, I lost my race with Carly.

It was only a stumble from station to water's edge. And there, under grim skies, with taciturn anglers and squabbling seagulls, commuters scurrying head-down and promenaders casting curious glances, I tugged off my dusty hiking boots, stripped off my socks, and bared my feet.

For my niece.

Until after eleven-thirty.

Rest & Recuperation
Sinead Reilly

I'm not sure what time it is. Late. I can tell because I can't hear any cars passing by. I usually can. Shadows of the tree outside my window are spilling across my ceiling. I can hear nothing save for the wind.

I concentrate on trying to lie perfectly still in the dark. I can't remember it ever being this dark. The sheer curtains are being swept about.

I am starting to feel as though I am floating in a tank when I register the first yelp. An animal. I think it's a cat, but upon hearing it again, it's clearly a dog. Must be my neighbour's dog—the young guy a bit further up. Don't know his name. The place that separates our houses has been vacant for a time. A nice young couple lived there long enough to realise they probably needed better. That was about a year ago, and the 'For Sale' sign is still up. Sunburnt now, peeling round the edges, and the photos are all faded too.

I try to listen more closely. The shadows continue to gambol about on the ceiling. If I don't blink, they get bigger and bigger.

After a few minutes I hear another whine. It's not really a whine, but I don't know how else to describe it. I haven't heard anything like it. I don't want to believe that it's a dog making that sound. A flurry of barks every so often means I can't fool myself much longer. The neighbours on the other side don't have any pets. Just the one guy there alone for as long as I've been here and probably twenty years more. I shouldn't be able to hear the dog from here.

Only minutes have passed before I hear it again. And again. The furiously dancing patterns, faster and faster, falling into and over each other—extricating contorting unfolding—transfix my sight in the still dark. Again. I shut my eyes.

I try to think of the last time I saw the dog. Can't think of her name, or how she looked. I know she's a retriever, white gold one. I like those ones. The yellow ones are alright. I can't think of whether I ever asked her name or how old she is or when the neighbour brought her home or anything much at all. Closing my eyes hasn't done much good at all. It's still going.

When I wake, the birds outside my window are calling to each other. They sound listless this morning. Feeble. They're probably not because birds can't really be listless or feeble unless they're sick or dying but maybe they can be. An ex-girlfriend of mine kept a parrot that always looked sort of miserable. Pulled out a bunch of its feathers once. She said it was stressed. I ended up letting it out the window and it probably didn't last much longer after that.

The sky is strewn with watery ink and some thin clouds, and acid from my stomach coats the back of my throat.

Fast-forward three blank months and I can remember little else but the sound of the dog getting kicked—which now seems optimistic—half to death every Friday night. I don't know why it only happens on Fridays. I don't think there is a reason. The guy could just clock off work and go have some beers like everyone else, but that doesn't seem to be on his agenda.

Strewn between the melting months have been increasingly desperate attempts to get a hold of someone at the police station who won't promise a call back, and then not call back.

I get through.

I don't want to fixate on what the woman sounded like, or even what she said when I asked why they haven't been answering the phone. I don't even think I asked. Not important. I was just happy that someone finally picked up. The voice—Carolina, I wrote it down—informed me that two officers will visit my neighbour's house on Thursday. Today is Sunday.

I told her that the dog gets beat up on Fridays—a visit on Thursday might be too late. What if he's not home, what if he's at work or the supermarket or takes his car to the mechanic? He has a job, he works, it's a nine-to-five job, and that's all I know. I haven't spoken to the guy much but he does work and he goes out after work too. He really isn't home that much, but I also don't know because I don't keep tabs on what the guy does at every waking moment, but maybe I should if they can't arrange to visit after five or earlier in the week—

Carolina asks me to please calm down. She's chewing gum. I want to hang up but there's a good chance that the dog would be in the ground by the time I manage to get through again.

I say thank you, make sure the officers do visit, thank you and goodbye.

Pieces of broken glass swim innocently in water on my kitchen floor. It's spattered all over the bit of paper I'd written my neighbour's address on. I watch as the letters bleed into each other slowly. It's sodden. I don't remember smashing the glass.

Trying not to think about the retriever, I pick up the slivers of glass and clean the water up. Snowy white fur matted with dark blood. My hands are shaking a little. Big soft ears.

Today is Thursday, and I've taken the day off work. Predictably, my neighbour is gone already. I need a day off anyway. I pace around my house and yard, caged, waiting for the officers to turn up as per Carolina's bidding.

I wait all day.

At around three, a flock of schoolgirls glide down the street. Snatches of their laughter float in through my windows.

They don't show up.

I wake in the early hours of Friday morning to the shrieks of the dog. My neighbour has tweaked his schedule slightly. Rest and recuperation. I lie in bed awhile with some music turned up full volume, trying not to picture violent things happening to the neighbour.

Getting into my car, I drive through the night until the hard dark sky is tempered a little by the dawn. Settling on radio voices talking about nothing much in particular, I turn the volume up to maximum and put all the windows down. The cool wind whips through the car and stays with me and I can't hear the voices talking at me at all.

Eventually I pull over by someone's field. The house is all dark and far away.

Ducking through the barbed wire fence, I lie down in the long grass. I don't know why people bother with barbed wire. The ground has been softened by rain and I'm trespassing. I have to get back in time for work but the sunrise is coming up all embarrassed pink and lunchbox yellow and the retriever's ears and snowy bloody fur.

Friday night is, unusually, something of a respite. Wonder what's up with him.

The following morning, I wait for my neighbour to go to work. He's listening to some pop rubbish as he drives away. I guess the wailing voices help drown out his conscience.

Tucking some old blankets under my arm, I turn down the narrow pathway leading to his backyard from the street. I didn't know how many I'd need so I brought them all. The front gate is abnormally small, so I push it open with my foot. I let myself into the backyard via the cracked path beside the house.

It takes me a few minutes to find her. She's in the shed and can't walk on her own. I think some of her bones must be broken. Gingerly, I wrap her up in the blankets and she whines with pain when I pick her up off the stained concrete. She's feather light, much too light. I'm sorry, I'm sorry, I'm sorry. Liquid brown eyes look up at me as I carry her down the street with soft steps. The pavement feels warm under my feet, radiating through my shoes and into my legs.

The vet asks a lot of pointed questions. I don't blame him.

Later, at home, I carefully wash her snowy fur. I'm lathered up to my elbows in red soapy foam. I gently towel her dry, smiling beatifically all the while.

After a couple of days go by, my neighbour knocks on the door. One-two-three.

I briefly consider ignoring it before deciding otherwise. I don't want him to get any ideas.

He's smiling one of those smiles where you can see all the teeth, and his hair is matted to his forehead a bit. I instantly want to close the door. He tells me where he lives—as if I didn't know—and asks whether I've seen his dog. I think a moment before shaking my head and telling him I'll keep an eye out.

Yeah, he says. Please do. He hasn't blinked this whole time. I close the door.

Friday

Rosanne Dingli

From the 1922 diary of Edith Kaufman

It will be dark soon. The lamps in the garden will come on, and everything out there will look quite different from the way it looks in the daytime, when sunlight turns all foliage a uniform green. The sun knows only one green, whereas the moon and those lamps show anyone lingering outside at this bewitching time a variety of shades. One comes equally close to glimpsing those hues on a sombre and overcast day, when a thousand greens, from lead grey to iceberg blue, populate the eye and bewilder the mind, just as one was about to bemoan the fact rain was on the way, or perhaps a gale.

Or perhaps a gale, which sends leaf litter from a morning's raking flying, and flattens foliage against these gelid window panes, just as they flattened that other Friday when your train was late, and, when it finally came in, blew litter about, and you were not on it.

No. You were not on it.

Carriages emptied quickly, with the haste of those hankering to be home, or longing to meet loved ones at last, or exhausted after a long journey and sick of being cooped up behind a pane showing only blurred countryside, spotted with cows and sheep and horses and more cows. And distant vanishing windows spangled with anonymous lights starting to come on in the gathering gloom.

The last alighting passenger clamped a quick hand to anchor his hat and disappeared. Dark soon.

Dark soon, but here darker than elsewhere. Perhaps where you are now the dark does not fall with as much portent as it does here; perhaps the greens you see are still vibrant with streaks of luminosity and sharpness.

Sharpness such as touches chestnut leaves, those long lanceolate things which twitch and shake to the touch. Which tremble when one passes, as we passed through and past and between and underneath those branches spreading so far and wide, so shadily and steadfast.

Steadfast.

Steadfast as perhaps one thought you might have become, until that telling empty carriage, those typical three or four carriages of a Western Australian country train, devoid of a soul and hissing off to shunt and return the other way. It left, in the gathering twilight, and on the platform remained this forlorn solitary form, wondering why surprise did not figure that evening. No—this was after all expected, foreshadowed, spoken about, even. It could end. One day it would be all over. It would finish, that which had happened between us.

'One Friday, I just might not be on the train.' Your voice so soft, and yet so troubling.

But so suddenly—so unannounced and without notice? Without even a word of warning or contrition or caution or apology? The expectation of politeness from one so graceful and gentle is reasonable. From one so poised and sophisticated, one expected a token of courtesy. Even if an understanding is secret, its keepers ought to maintain a degree of regard.

No note, no message. A quick leafing through the evening edition causes no commotion. Princess Mary is marrying her viscount. There is a hung parliament in Tasmania. A new art prize for portraits has been inaugurated. But here, scant light and no innovation or celebration stir the monotony of days.

So it is over. What there was between us is no longer. Such an ending requires a gesture. Words. Words which might have been spoken, on the telephone, in a brief and awkward sentence or two. Voices flattened by wires twisted over long miles. Or written, even, in a letter the like of which no one likes to receive, either suddenly and without notice, or with all the hints and warnings in the world.

Perhaps there were a dozen. A few, a scarce few hints. Six hundred. All the indications in the world. In this world of greying green. Of blackening shadows where twitches and shakes announce another of those windy nights. Now, when one does not care to venture out to smoke and pace on a driveway whose edges become hardly visible and whose length at last disappears into the distance of the avenue of peppermint trees planted by goodness knows which ancestor.

What ray of light remains?

These lamps signal a kind of hope in permanence, the kind of longevity one needs to do little to maintain. Requiring little thought or work they come on without fail each night, came on even that Friday, needing only the attention of a servant and a switch. And they gleam among a dozen muted greens, among the young growth of spring roses, among large spatulate leaves that are arum lilies whose white trumpets are still in the future, but whose cycle of perpetuity is reliable and reassuring. Among the jarrah trees you admired for their age and remarkable height.

In this world where little else is heartening, the moon is awaited for, and for sure, it rises over the fence which turns from its dark grey to gold.

Gold.

There was no gold on your fingers, nor around your neck. You desired and displayed the sort of plainness that only one so beautiful can carry off. And you knew it too, most probably because from infancy that truth was repeatedly in the mouths of adoring grandparents who taught you your style. In gardens of carefully planned colour, they planted foliage banks (you recounted and described), that turned not grey but silver, in the dying hours of day. And in your mind seeded ideas of art and literature equalled in weight and importance only by the music that reverberated through their tranquil rooms. Florence Ewart and Charles Packer on the radiogram, heard even out in that silver garden where no gales blew, and no frost ever ruined a single leaf.

But into each life some disaster must bring its mould or destruction, its decay and deterioration, and inevitably it arrived in yours. And not a word of it did you utter, but it showed in your eyes in brief flashes. Somehow there was the thought it might have been eased, repaired, by what happened between us this summer. Because there was a hint of joy, was there not? The faith was there that your dilemma might have been erased. The time it takes to travel between the railway station and this gravel driveway, however, has brought enough persuasion, enough of a conclusion, that it could not have done very much at all.

Nothing.

All that is left of a summer of walks in the garden of this place, through the reserve luckily saved from the avaricious grasp distant city offices tightened around the estate, through the bush that borders the Blackwood river at Bridgetown, and up around the small hill we used to call ours, all that is left is a hint of green. All is darkening around the pioneer cemetery we read like a book.

It is dark now, and another train must have arrived and left this evening, as it did that Friday, leaving the platform desolate and chilly, swept by a chill that will grip the valley all night.

All night, and until the darkest hour, and then the currents and breezes and draughts will shorten and sweep languidly and stop. Stop almost as suddenly as a heart does when a shock takes it fully by surprise. Cease to find a still dawn thrilling so very softly to the calls of several thousand birds. Each bird cries in diurnal attempts to outdo the others, heard through the din of the start of another day.

Full morning brings with it the press of tasks and duties and errands and responsibilities that hang around such a place as this. Things to be bought, things repaired, creatures to be cared for, and people who depend on a reliable routine, ordained by the folding and unfolding of countless yesterdays.

Yesterday.

Friday.

Today.

When on the platform at this station one waits again, this time for Mama, who arrives from Perth full of talk and smiles and comfort and consolation. Who arrives accompanied by a dozen (or so it seems) matching suitcases and a similar number of packages, and a proffered silver watch which always needs attention from someone a bit more knowledgeable of such things. So a smile is wrung from my lips and face, which struggle to conform. An embrace wrested from one demolished and wilted by an ending. An insurmountable emotion created by an arrival which never took place.

The place is greener than green, she says, this woman who has loved me a whole lifetime, with admiration cleverly taking the place of soppy childhood comfort, and turning into a kind of well-placed solace.

There are a dozen greens, from lead grey to iceberg blue, but today, today they are steel green and teal, nearly identical in the blazing sun.

Softening surely with the lengthening of shadows, from the presence of one so squashed and palpably defeated, she says there must be tea, darling, and gallons of it, to accompany conversation—words, words, words—

114

that will by the time the lamps come on, lead on to…to something. To changing for dinner and sitting at table, all cream and silver and porcelain white, suddenly captivated by elegance (because she is here) of a different style from yours. Or is it?

Or was it?

It is the grace of ages, the sophistication of time, which no doubt will be yours when you reach the decade that now so comfortably embraces Mama. This is the age she knows how to be; this is the comfort she knows how to bestow. Given, yet unspoken. Dealt, yet unmentioned. Magical, ethereal, like the perfect stage play whose wright knew everything knowable about care and generosity.

It will be dark soon. But here, garden lamps streak some of the foliage with gold, with the accompanying glow from the rising moon, whose dented shape ventures over the grey horizontals of the high fence.

The chairs are new. Yes, new chairs, and blacker in this light. Their angled silhouettes paint another kind of tracery, branches light and twiggish, leafless and ghostly, but full of a kind of reassurance that one does not buy new chairs in the spirit of hopelessness. One plans and attempts the design of a new garden, even now—a garden of flat glaucous fronds and white and orange flowers.

One plans.

And strikes a new balance, and converses with Mama of trains and roads and cars, which these days all look quite alike and indistinguishable, except perhaps for the Austin 7. They must be quite robust, and dependable, she supposes, and, to the modern eye, represent something of style and clever fashioning, those ugly cars. She concedes, and repeats, and makes a few clever jokes that hearten, and gladden. And mentions and suggests events to take place in this future garden, in this spot, replete with banksia and nuytsia.

An ache.

One realises with an ache that it is over.

Gone, what happened between us. It is ended, never to return, and the world has moved in, filling these spaces with silver and cream, with gold and green and the surprising scents of peppermint and eucalyptus.

It is dark. It is late. The used glasses can be left for the morning.

The Colonel
Vito Milana

{Summer 1855}

Finn's turbulent birth, propelled by the escalating cries of dying cicadas, came to pass on a windless Tuesday afternoon. The occasion is rather frenzied in an otherwise humdrum and unusually dry March. It is eighteen-hundred and fifty-five—in the year of the Lord—on the brink of Van Diemen's Land's inevitable demise. The ostensibly nonchalant and childless Colonel stands miserably tall and watches the trunk where his swollen wife, fading fast, continues to cry. She is slumped at the base of the smooth-gummed eucalyptus and is riddled with fragility, unable to be moved indoors. The wife had collapsed, only moments earlier, while sweeping away withered leaves and gathering some of the rescuable fallen fruit.

The pair live isolated on the outskirts of Deloraine, a township scattered along the Meander River which has been fitfully explored these recent years. They arrived from the Great Western Tiers, amidst growing uncertainties, just shy of twenty months ago. To the north of their flaking weatherboard home lies a dehydrated and sunlit patch settled within the ruins of several neglected garden beds and pockets of mud. The Colonel's prematurely aged hands failed at reviving the dying produce and the wife was often too bothered by the lack of shade and the sickly summery heat to tend to the fractured soil. It now remains a flounced clearing with a handful of pecking fowl and partially buried treasures of the couple's recent past: some musket firing balls, a splintered bucket with stains of speckled water shadows, and a threadbare cloth.

Behind the woman's arch lies a tattered *Hobart Town Gazette* half-hidden amongst the baked and rotting citrus, and the ink has puddled under her salty sweat. The Colonel looks away and shuffles uncomfortably in his boots. They carry a warring dust that bursts northerly with every slight movement.

A handful of minutes scatter by, and with the rising wind and the heron's desperate flight Finn is born—and with the swiftly sinking sun, so too the mother departs. She rests in her watery blood and her eyelids softly shut. *What an unprecedented exchange,* the Colonel wallows, and he cradles his son and gently ushers the servant girl away. A quiet settles in the corridor of the eve as the wind abandons its whistle and the landscape calms. The Colonel bends his confused frame and removes her Irish cross, a moment of quiet contemplation flooding his gaze. He then stands, Finn close in embrace, and stoically crosses his chest. He closes his bushed and clouded eyes.

A sombre sonnet, a sketchy and ginger memory, returns the Colonel to his English childhood. A mosaic of colours thread together to form the vision of yesteryear and a forgotten tenderness. He captures his mother's gaze as she fattens the fire with wood. The Colonel hears her voice, so fragrant, and whistles along to the words:

For sweet is the grass near yesterday's squall
A memory, a memory, for me
The men with the guff and drink on their shoulders
A memory, a memory, to see
And the wintry leaves flee to scatter tomorrow
A memory, a memory for me
Oh such are days that fall all around me
A memory, a memory, to be

{Summer 1863}
The slumbering child squeezes his knees tight. Despite the glowing fire-warmth that blankets the town, there is an unshakeable cold on Finn's wrinkled feet, and goosebumps invade his bare skin. His ghostly mother's face embraces his sleep and Finn's lips curl into a smile. It is all too familiar, this quiet exchange between the deceased mother and her living child, and he is not concerned about her silent reply. Her image is captured, fleetingly, and his rapid breathing intensifies. *Mother,* he wheezes in whispered ecstasy. Fragility consumes her face and her eyes swell with astonishment. *Marvelous Finn,* she mouths, inaudibly, and drifts out into the drying dreamscape.

The vision then swiftly fades and the emptiness signals wakefulness in young Finn. This is immediately followed by the arrival of a violent thud beyond the bedroom's wall. The arresting aroma of cooked leather boots, sordid perfume, and an impudently charmless tune assaults his senses. The child reactively stirs.

The crack of the pistol sharpens the early morning calm and Finn knows that the Colonel has returned. He barrels into Finn's room, draped in booze, and gestures at the woman attached to his side. She is a failed Catholic with miserable lipstick, a stocky stature and a thirst for salvation.

My son, the Colonel grunts, and licks his needle teeth. Finn watches the lady's intoxicated and glazed stare.

As the couple bury their way up the hall, he wonders how many hours of rum have run through his father, or if this time, perhaps, it was whiskey that had danced in his throat. He sighs as the Colonel erupts into bursts of unmelodic laughter and swigs from a bottle. The pair stagger into the adjacent bedroom and Finn hears the violent slamming of timber, a fabric's tear, a muffled cry, and, finally, a quiet. He is unperturbed by the frenzied arrival, the third in as many days.

A welcomed warm breeze arrives and Finn, nearly eight, covers his belly, yawns, and scratches his skin. He closes his eyes and wills and waits but his mother fails to return that Christmas morn.

{Winter 1872}

A decade floats by and the pervading chill of 1872 arrives. Finn shivers. He is underdressed in a threadbare jacket and patchy brown trousers. His shoes are the tattered products of coarse repairing and his socks are darkened and frayed. Finn clutches his luggage, rather light, and secures the Bible under his arm. He lifts his spare hand and, with frozen fingers, tucks a lock of hair behind his ears and catches a cloud to the east. The mother's cross, timeworn, adorns his neck. The Launceston–Deloraine train draws near and Finn's ticket is checked.

The Colonel had followed his son up the footworn road, shuffling behind like a mangy dog. *You are afflicted!* Finn suddenly shouts, aboard the train, brazen-faced and choked. A hoard of clouds threatens above and shoulder the arrival of a greying darkness. The teenager's dreary eyes blink and he prepares for a final exchange. A taste like bitter fruit builds in his mouth and he spits to the fresh Tasmanian earth. *We are all afflicted,* barks the Colonel in return and, withered, hobbles away.

The emotion quickly evaporates and Finn recomposes his slender frame. Two heart-sick fishermen, gaunt, stand transfixed in the shade and Finn, thunderstruck by an unexpected melancholy, swallows his thoughts. The train departs.

{Summer 1884}

The years fatten by and, with the arrival of '84, Finn reaches 29. He has warmed to Lithgow: the settlement spilling towards the gentility of the Blue Mountains' plump terrain. Finn's companions are few and he carries memories of a failed relationship into the new year. She had the most extraordinary face, gentle features and a spirited smile. They were consumed by a brief but electric friendship and entertained one another with passion and drink. Yet they quickly suffered amongst differences and, one chaotic afternoon, she vanished.

The Colonel had then died and Finn drank himself comatose—an attempt at self-preserved solidarity—but reached no salvation. Instead, he had awoken the following afternoon, felt awfully hungry, and took to smoking cigarettes. The monotony of each day on the mainland meandered by and Finn felt escalating solace in his commitment to aloneness and regular bouts of hard work.

Thursday eve arrives and Finn's butcher knife lowers—the howl of the final beast ceases as the abattoir dries for another day. It is spectacularly warm and Finn expels a seasonal sigh while dusting his hands into the fleecing breeze. The nails are discoloured and there is fever across his skin.

Homeward bound with the company of fat flies, Finn scratches the dried blood on his arm and notices a pair of ants scurry towards his thumb. He cradles the offcuts, double-wrapped in scotched paper and tightly held together with cotton string, and shields the package from the ever hungry circling birds. A white gum greets him ahead and he notices its fading bark and flaky skin. Finn marvels at the hills and scattering of livestock. *They are surviving well*, he reflects, and raises his meal to defend himself from the punishing sun.

Reaching the porch, he digs his hands deep into the belly of the house and draws out a polished bottle from the cool damp of the darkened space. He discards the cork and empties the contents while shuffling inside. The motion is sweeping and, as Finn peels away his reddened and muddied

119

wears, another follows.

The thicket of night blankets the hills and Finn drags his frame outside to stare at the cauliflower-white moon. With squinting eyes and baked sweat on his brow and under his pits, he tramples a collection of half-blown dandelions and bites his lower lip. The pebbled road erupts with splintered shards following the thunderous smash of glass and Finn, cracked into a grin, raises his almighty arms to the spiritless sky. A blue air rises from the earth and circles the swaying butcher, as the familiar prayers of cicadas commence. The uncooked pieces of meat are forgotten and slump on the porch. A pair of empty-bellied kookaburras peck apart the wrapping and tear away at the drying flesh.

{Autumn 1887}

A stale quiet lingers outside the church following Sunday's longer than usual worship. Finn is irritated by the imposition and, some moments later, the barking catechism on divine manifestation ceases to ring in his ears. He holds his wife tight, lusts for her caress, and they walk home under the guide of the autumnal breeze. Crisp leaves stir underfoot and unripe green-yellow lemons litter the path.

Finn's seemingly unquenchable thirst swiftly arrives, but he shelves the thoughts and begins burying in the garden. Dirt captures under his nails. Cloth under arm, whistle in her cheeks, Oyster Bay pine by the frame, Finn's wife busies under the trampled midmorning. She meanders down the hall towards the barren table and wipes the ceramic cups clean.

Finn stands and washes the hardship from his hands and gingerly removes his boots. Rising aromas of boiled beef, spiced potatoes and misty caramelised onions fill his nostrils and lift his tired mood. They embrace, slowly, near the open fire and he heatedly whispers in her ears. Finn watches her, breathlessly. She smiles, presses her lips to his arm, and strokes his charcoal hair. It is seven o'clock and the sun begins its descent to coincide with the death of the day.

It is 10 o'clock and the home is washed and absorbed in faint night. A new moon sky peers through the window's crack and bathes the chair a dusty silver. *And you...*Finn accuses agitatedly, stumbles, and cradles the bottle against his splashed shirt. His cheeks are an extraordinary plum-blood red and he tries, hopelessly, to fix his wavering eyes to meet his wife's stare. Finn nurses his neck and clicks his fingers wildly in front of her. Belligerent and ignoble, he slurs and falls backwards with an almighty thud. The bottle bounces and empties on the rug. Finn's bottom lip begins a spasmodic quiver and his wife, somewhat annoyed, glances down at him commiseratingly. She patters up the tight-walled hallway to settle in.

{Summer 1893}

The third daughter, unnamed, passes away into the quiescent eve. The industrial sound from the blast furnace blends with the cries at Cox's River as wet summer rain continues to stir. The tiny body is buried with her sisters and the wife is quickly ushered inside.

A broken 38-year-old Finn settles down with another bottle. *Happy New Year* he attests, with a puzzled plastered smile, and picks at his beard. He snaps back his head and tosses his mother's cross into the open rain.

{Winter 1894}

A gaunt Finn wakes alone. His wife's poorly feathered pillow remains warm and the scent of her lingers. And lingers still.

Get it off Your Chest

Tyler Heesh

21 February

Dear friend,

J. always said start with the lie you want to believe, stare that in the face, and then work your way towards the truth.

… I know. 'Insinuations without accusations'…let me try again.

21 February

Dear friend,

J. always said start with the half of the story you know, and then stare the question 'What am I missing?' in the face.

Last week, O. was trying to describe you with an idiom, but ended up botching it in their typical way, saying you 'have your ear on the pulse.' They're not wrong. You seem to know everything about everyone. I admire how you use that information: to help people get jobs; to get us to ask someone, 'How are you?' but in the deep, won't take a default answer kind of way; to point out who we need to drop everything to love.

I often think of when H. & I broke up and you stayed with me. So many people dropped by my house and left gifts. I didn't say it then, but I knew your hands were behind all of it, even the dubious roast chicken with the heavily discounted price tag.

And yet…this letter is me asking…what if I'm missing something?

… you'd hate this too…I remember being in the car with you, looking out at the ocean, eating sour straps, dissolving into some music about how things used to be. 'Just tell me the truth if it's the truth,' you said …

27 February

Dear friend,

A few months ago B. said they were hanging out with their family when they realised 'everyone is a gossip in their own way.' That anecdote stuck with me. I love knowing everyone's information, and, even more sinister, I love other people knowing I know everyone's information.

I wonder if this is the same for you?

… Is this a bit too disingenuous? What I really want is to speak to you, not speak to you through illuminating my own failings, though they certainly exist…When we hear something which could be important for ourselves, too often our instinct is 'I know who needs to hear this' and the 'who' is never us. I remember the other day someone (one of the only people I know who you don't!) told me they were getting a new job before some of our mutual friends knew. So I practiced the face I would use when they announced it at a lunch we had to show that I already knew. How messed up is that?

2 March

Dear friend,

Thank you for the audiolog today. I can't imagine using my time on the train home from work so generously. It was just so timely.

There is something beautiful about being known. H. said the point at which they would be ready to get married is when someone knew them more than their parents did.

And really, no one knows me more than you. You've been there for it all:

- You went to that board game tournament with me despite the fact you suck at board games
- When H. & I broke up, you were there almost instantly…and had you known that episode would lead to food poisoning, you would still choose to do it all over again
- You paid for my ticket to go to the Philippines with my family and visit my great grandma, and you came too after Lola invited you
- I don't think I've felt a peace like that time we sat by the beach when we'd really realised uni was over

You know how I could go on. I suppose this letter is my way of saying… thank you for being the person in my life who knows me best.

… sigh…this whole time I have been trying to write something I feel

123

you need to hear, and you so regularly diagnose what I value and give me what I need to hear.

13 March
Dear friend,

I contemplated sharing about all the times I've tried to write this letter with you today when we were talking by the pond about whether people trust others more if they're funny. You'd probably ask, 'Why would you hesitate to say something if it's the truth?'

I suppose my fear is that sharing my insecurities with you will ruin something between us. But the truth probably is that in not sharing, in failing to be honest, there could be something far more ruinous.

As you read this, please remember that something we are good at is being present with one another in the mess. You have so much time for me, today being another example of that, and none of what comes below can undermine that reality.

Every day I …

… this sucks…I'm just imagining you sending me that article about how gossip is good for you and promotes behavioural reform. That's probably not a fair estimation of how you'd react, but why am I expecting a piece of paper to change anything?

7 April
J,

I know I haven't written to you in so long. I don't know if I'm ready to feel guilty about that.

I saw Lola today. I never told you this, but her mum had cancer. She died a month and a half ago. I'm sad Great Grandmother's gone, sad that cancer even exists, sad to have no living connection to where Lola grew up. And somehow I'm possibly—and I hope you believe that line B. says about grief not being linear—more sad about a single moment from today.

We had family breakfast. Lola was teary about not visiting her mother in the last few weeks of her life. When Lola was in the kitchen making tea, another family member said, 'If she really wanted to see her mum, she should have gone. Doesn't matter how expensive the flights were.'

To take an opinion about someone else's life and shout it so pointedly to the group of people whose opinions Lola cares about most, without her

124

even knowing. Why? What insecurity are you protecting by sharing that? I never want to share anything of myself with them. The water will never flow that way again.

This game we all play where we think we know what's best for other people's lives and we don't do anything about it, except maybe to talk to some random third person—and in many cases fourth, fifth, sixth—about it…I'm so sick of it. How much of the oxygen, how much of the art in this world, is expended on triangulation?

What would it look like for things to be different?

Maybe I just need to talk to that family member. But I haven't even been able to talk to someone I care far more deeply for. It's probably inadvisable to share this with you, but I'm trying to write someone a letter because I can't stop thinking of one moment where I wish they had stayed silent …
Love,

8 April

Dear friend,

I wish I lacked the awareness to consider how for everything going on in the world, this is what I am choosing to write about in this moment. I know. I feel the weight of my narrow-mindedness. Maybe that's cause enough to ignore the contents below.

Although, do you remember how J. used to say one of my biggest failings was going too macro? Someone would talk about a decision and my instinct was, 'But if they do this now, what kind of person are they deciding to be in the future?' and J. would say, 'Oh no, not this non-consequentialism thing again.'

They just wanted someone to love them. 'They go micro, you go the universe.' So maybe instead of feeling the burdens of the planet here, I try to love the person in front of me. And I hope you do see this as love. Love doesn't mean affirmation of everything. You know this. You taught me this.

Every day I wish you didn't share with people that H. and I were close to getting engaged.

But please don't take the point to be that you messed up this one time, or that I am lamenting that relationship and the way things broke down.

Rather, maybe this kind of stuff makes me lament our relationship. I feel like such a fool when I think about you sitting on the couch of our friend's share-house with paintings of doves or hillsides or whatever that stupid artwork is, letting go of words that don't belong to you, to people whose joy or sadness could have been fuller had they heard it from the source. I haven't cried in you know how long, but that image makes me wish I did cry.

... nope...emotional. Unfair...and it probably says more about me than you?

29 April
Dear friend,

Thank you for hanging out today. Thank you for the cake. I'm sorry the waterfalls we picked were drier than those songs made them out to be. Thanks for sticking with me when I am inconsistent, especially in grief.

The other day a few of us were trying to think of things that were 'good and bad.' We talked about bipartisanship and air travel and sparkling water.

I kept thinking about you. I envy the way you are unafraid to launch in and be with people in their hardships. You do good with what you know about people. But maybe your lack of hesitation to love is what enables you to hurt people.

This letter is my way of encouraging you to realise that maybe you can be one without the other.

And maybe I need to see that in you, in order to believe it could be true of me. Because maybe I'm just a broken version of you?

... I give up

15 May
Dear friend,

Can you stop, as O. says, 'Spilling the cat out of the bag'? Please. Those cats don't always belong to you.

Which makes me think perhaps we love to gossip because we love to belong.

... Why can't I just say it? Why can't I just be angry or sad or anything without some reflection about the world or myself overflowing onto the page?

17 June

J,

Another letter where I reflect on something in my life. You'd probably be wondering why I haven't asked about you.

Yesterday I went for a walk with B. We were circling the harbour, talking about how fragile certain periods of life are and how they can end, or continue, in an instant. They live in a share-house. They were telling me that when the house needed to move it was complicated because it looked like one of their housemates was going to get engaged, and then they didn't. The conversation moved on. I finished my matcha. We said goodbye. I cried in the car. I bought another parking ticket so I could cry in the car for a half hour longer. I just...hearing someone talk about someone else's personal stuff and not using their name or identifying features ...

I really need to send this letter ...

Lola used to tell this story about rice farmers being able to see water at the tops of the mountain before their springs would overflow, promising the end of the drought. I miss how time with you felt like being filled up.

Love,

18 June

Dear friend,

I wanted to share two things with you:

1) You care about me more than anyone else has ever cared about me, more than H., more than J.

2) Every day, I wish I got to hear it from J. first that her cancer had recurred.

Love,

23 June

J,

I did two things recently:

1) I mailed the letter to my friend

2) I threw away the CD I bought for you the day before I found out your cancer came back. I'm so sorry I never gave it to you.

Love,

The Bone Pearl

Keshe Chow

This is how I remember my grandmother: knee-deep in water, skirts knotted around her waist. Her crow's feet crinkling, feathers woven through her wispy hair.

We're gathering oysters down on Half Moon Bay. She's the type of grandmother who is always rationing, always trying to glean food from the earth. Wading through the shallows, she bends over, bird-like, sifting through piles of clacking shells. She plucks a shell from the bottom of the sea bed. Straightens. Holds it in her palm.

'Here, child,' she says, beckoning me over. 'Tell me what you hear.'

I'm a little too old for this, I think. But I do it anyway, only rolling my eyes internally.

She settles the shell over my ear, dampening all external sound. Salt air pricks my nostrils. I breathe in, then out, the air rushing across my tongue like the tide. Then I close my eyes, and *listen*.

I hear the heartbeat of my mother's womb. I hear time stretching backward, morphing through millennia. I hear the first cry of a human baby, the first bird song to greet the dawn. I hear planets turning, atoms forming, nebulae swirling through the vacuum of space. I hear the sun, the moon, fragmented rocks.

I hear everything.

'Well?' My grandmother arches a wiry brow, the faintest smile playing about her lips.

Afraid, I slap the shell from my head and duck away. 'The sea, Wai Po,' I lie, my mouth dry, like sand. 'All I hear is the sea.'

When I was younger, I used to play with shells on the bed while Wai Po rearranged her pearls. So many pearls, all strung on different lengths of string—some as white as fresh-fallen snow, others deep blue, as dark as the sea. I remember begging her to let me touch them, play with them. Usually she said no. Occasionally, though, she would say yes.

The pearls, she'd say, *are a penance. Payment for my services.*

'What services?' I would ask in my eight-year-old innocence. But she never replied.

My grandmother lived alone, somewhat apart from the village. I called her Wai Po, but the locals called her nu wu.

Witch.

She wasn't a witch, not really. At least I didn't think so. What she did was help people, heal people.

Specifically, she helped women. They would come to her—materialising from the bottomless nights—and shut themselves in her bedroom for hours, whispering. When they emerged, as though from a chrysalis, they would press pearls into my grandmother's palm and kiss her papery cheek. I always noticed they seemed less substantial, more translucent, as though the colour was slowly leaching from their bodies.

Then they would disappear. Gone from the village to be never seen again. Black birds would come, harbingers of gloom, gathering on fence posts and the rooftops of houses. After such events people would speak of monsters, of demons, and continue hissing the word.

Witch.

I hated it. I *hated* it. I knew Wai Po was helping those women, but rumours still clung to my skin. I hated how folks stared whenever I walked down the street; how they'd surreptitiously pace wide arcs to avoid me. Most of all I hated the other children. The way they teased me, spat on me.

'Witch!' they would taunt, throwing rocks at my feet. 'Spawn of a witch!'

When I asked my grandmother about it on one of my daily visits, she said to ignore them. The women, she said, were not disappearing.

They were *escaping*.

'Escaping from what?' I asked.

My grandmother lowered herself onto the bed, bracing herself with her hands on her knees. 'Fetch one of those, child,' she said, pointing to one of her pearl necklaces nestled inside a velvet box.

I picked it up, feeling the disproportionate weight of it in my fingers.

Scrambling onto the bed behind her, I fastened it around her neck.

'Do you know that pearls are made of pain?' she said, the consonants languid, coating the flat of her tongue.

'What do you mean, Wai Po?' I replied, stroking the smooth spheres, watching the way the light refracted around the lustre.

My grandmother chuckled, then shook her head. 'It is difficult to explain,' she said. 'Next time we gather oysters, let me show you.'

Next time was nearly a week later. By the time we made our descent to the beach, I was almost jumping from my skin.

'Show me,' I said, bouncing on my toes. 'Show me now?'

My grandmother splashed into the shallows, her eyes trained on the water, peering past the shattered light and the darting schools of fish. I carefully rolled up the hems of my trousers and followed her into the sea.

Finally, she spotted what she was looking for. Her hand plunged into the ice-cold water, closing around a teardrop shell. It was wet, glistening, the outside steeped in oil-slick colour.

'Mother of Pearl.' Wai Po grinned, taking a blunt knife from her pocket. She levered open the shell and presented it to me.

I looked down and gasped. Sitting in the center of the butterflied shell was a perfect, burnished pearl.

My eyes wide, I asked her, 'How did this get here?' With her encouragement, I plucked it out of the shell and held it in my hand, its warm weight pressing against the creases of my palm.

The skin around Wai Po's eyes crinkled, obscuring the whites of her eyes. 'It is made by the oyster, qīn ài de.' She extended one finger and touched it, very gently. 'When the oyster feels pain, such as a shard of sand, it does not fall to pieces. It does not die, or resign itself to its suffering. Instead'—here she wrapped her hand around mine, curling the pearl inside my fist—'it makes something beautiful. Can you imagine? Something so beautiful coming from pain?'

I clutched it to my chest. 'Does beauty always come from pain, Wai Po?' I asked. But grandmother was already wading back to shore.

Over time, I stopped visiting my grandmother so often. Life got in the way, then friends, then school. And as I grew, the bullies' taunts began to dig into my skin, working their way under my membrane, my epidermis, right into my chest. Lodging there like a shard of sand.

At times, I wished I had a way of making pearls. Of hardening my heart to the gossip, the rumours, the backhanded insults. The nasty giggles from behind cupped hands. But I quickly realised that my grandmother had spoken nonsense. Beauty never came from pain. Not my pain, anyway. All pain did was eat me from the inside until I was as hollow and as resonant as a discarded, empty shell.

Sometimes, I'd stomp to Wai Po's house after school, my head engulfed by whatever dark, nucloud that had accumulated that day. I would ask—no, demand—she stop helping those women, stop making them disappear. 'They think you're a witch, Wai Po. A *witch*! Don't you see? Why can't you just be *normal*?'

Grandmother would just smile benignly and shake her head. 'I am sorry, bâobèi,' she'd say. 'I cannot stop. One day, it will be you. One day you will understand.'

I got so absorbed in my childish woes that I never noticed my grandmother's health deteriorating. It didn't occur to me that she shuffled more slowly, or that her shoulders were more bent, or that she didn't often go oyster-gathering down at the beach anymore. All that mattered was that people judged her, and hence me, behind our backs. I tried to close myself off to the whispered words, tried pressing both hands over my ears in order to shut out the sounds. But I still heard them. The insults always found their way in, piercing holes in my hands as though they were paper—not bone and skin and flesh.

The last time I ever saw my grandmother, I yelled at her. Screamed at her. 'Why can't you stop? Why is *your* work more important than *my* happiness? I don't want this, I never asked for this.' I took a deep breath. 'You know what? I don't want *you*!'

I snatched up my school bag, shouldering it with unnecessary force, and stomped my way out her door.

I didn't look around, but felt her eyes boring into my back regardless.

The news comes early one morning. My mother shakes me awake. I'm groggy as I push my hands into the arms of the robe she is holding.

Outside, the sky is still untouched by dawn.

My mother bundles me into the back of the car and, crossing the shadows of the waning night, we drive the short, three minute drive to my grandmother's house.

'What's going on?' I ask as we enter, but Māma shushes me. Wai Po's house is dark, too dark. And quiet. Normally she snores. Why does she not snore?

'Mā,' I say, my voice rising. 'Why are we here? Where is Wai Po?'

My mother turns to me, the sheen of tears rendering her sclera shiny, like a pearl. 'Oh, darling,' is all she says.

I run to my grandmother's room, which is shrouded in darkness. Her bed clothes are rumpled. The pillows still bear an impression of her head. But she's not there. Her nightgown is beside her bed, puddled on the floor. And outside the open window I spy a small black speck. A bird, winging its way toward the low-lying moon.

Grandmother's pearl case is lying open, empty. When I pick it up, my fingers brush against the pale velvet, darkening it to a fleshy pink. The case falls from my fingers, hitting the floor with a crash.

Where are all the pearls?

Their absence strikes me harder than Wai Po's empty bed. I want to cry, scream, claw at my chest. But I don't. Instead I run, pushing past my mother, slamming up against the waves of her grief until I'm completely, utterly suspended in my own.

When I finally stop running, salt air whips my hair and cools my tear-laced cheeks. The egg yolk sun cracks over the horizon, touching my face with its gilded light.

Half Moon Bay. I had thought I was running aimlessly, but my feet... they took me here.

Charging into the ocean, I let the water disperse my tears. When I put my head under, the sound is muffled. Waves crash and fizzle across my broken shell of skin.

By the time I trudge back to my grandmother's house, I am soaked.

It's then that I see it. A small black bird, its chest caved in, half-hidden in the folds of Wai Po's empty gown. And nestled inside its ribcage: a single, perfect, luminescent pearl.

Did you know, Wai Po once said, *that pearls are made of pain?*

I didn't know, Grandmother. I didn't know before. But now I do.

Pain isn't something that comes from outside. It is, and always has been, something internal.

Something personal.

I used to think of pain like barbs, spearing my skin until it was riddled with holes. Little did I know it was the pain on the inside—sequestered within my own shiny shell—that would fester, that would rot. That would break me, eventually.

Tears flash down my face like diamonds. I squint through their hazy veil.

It hadn't been the universe I'd first heard inside that shell. It was my own fragile heartbeat, my pulse, the sound of my blood rushing through my chest. My scream echoing through my body until all I could hear was my own mind screaming back.

'I understand now, Wai Po,' I whisper, plucking out the pearl. The pain was always from me. Within me. The grit that makes the pearl.

I take this pearl, this pearl of pain, and add it to my own.

Hermit's Hut

Kerry Munnery

The hut slumped against a granite wall, half hidden by bracken and saplings. The Park Ranger, a young woman with a cap pulled tight over her long dark braid, almost didn't see it. Maeve was mulling solutions to a tree fallen across the walking trail a couple of hundred metres away when a rosella burst from a *Hedycarya* to her right, drawing her attention to an arrangement of lines that was not quite organic. Intrigued, she stepped off the path.

The wood of the hut was weathered to silver, slowly splitting either side of old iron nails. The planks showed rough edges hacked and shaped by a crude axe, the head of which lay by the remains of a stump overgrown with fungi and moss into a mottled mound.

Maeve paused in the doorway. It was the end of a cool autumn day and already the light was diminishing. She had taken too long out here, deep in the Otways National Park, savouring her solitude. The earthy smell from the muddy humus under her feet and the lime-green curl of new fern fronds always invoked her childhood in Wombat River, a gentle creek that ran into a little bay off the Great Ocean Road. It wasn't until high school that she truly understood that not all children walked to waterfalls before breakfast and ended the day paddling in rockpools at sunset.

She took out her torch and guided it over the crude interior of the hut. Everything inside was made from wood. Table and bench, shelves, three legged stool. All mossy, mottled, damp, but well preserved. There was a moment when she instinctively backed away, as you might when you stumble into a scene too private for witnesses. Like cool air from a cave, the small space exuded an intense sense of intimacy. Her thin, sharp light scraped along a pale tangle in the corner—a rib cage, a skull, teeth.

The man had walked away from the infant city carrying things that could be described singly—cup, blanket, hammer. Walked until he came at sunset to a rock wall of matching colours, purple and pale apricot and grey and cream, and stopped and warmed his fingertips on the stone. In front of the rock, a small clearing was being kept tidy by kangaroos, needing only the pulling of a few flimsy bracken stems to clear it, the brushing away of the kangaroo scats, the stomping of dirt into a few rough holes with a heavy boot.

He stood in the middle of the small clearing and listened to the silence that was not silence, but the absence of city-noise, and then began. The trees remained trees until he cut them, and they became planks when he shaped them, and the planks nailed together were a hut, and the hut became his home because he lived in it. The words followed his hands in the proper manner.

The hut was shaped to his needs and, like his needs, it was stronger than it appeared at first glance. Not that there was anyone to see it, this far out in the bush. There was no one to raise an eyebrow and declare the hut slovenly or rustic or charming. The man had fled this sort of confusion, the way words piled up around an object until he lost the idea of what was right in front of him, lost the idea of himself even, under their weight. Lost what he had thought was his when he signed his name in black strokes to a paper he could not read and then could not understand the explanation of why this was right and just.

The man had been a carpenter there and had managed to keep all his tools. Now he lived surrounded by shaped wood. He took his time to carve boughs into a golden plate and goblet and bowl. He only needed one of each and had all the time he wanted to take. Early efforts that did not please his eye could be burned to roast his dinner.

Every day he tended to the hut, closing chinks as they appeared, propping up a corner, slicing a new shingle to patch the roof. Every day he disappeared into the forest and returned with dead animals, and every night the hut took him in without judgment or comment. There were no words, but it was far from silent. The nights were noisy with the throaty chuckles of possums and the days with the chirrups and moans and squeaks of birds he identified only by their cries.

And the days came and went, shorter and colder, and longer and milder, stacking like logs into seasons and building into years, and they grew into each other, the hut and the man. The man was the hut's god and creator, the hut was part of the man's skin and the only audience for his rare speech.

At last the man curled up into a corner he had hammered together himself, glad of the tight meeting of planks that held him and returned his warmth. The sun shone through the open door into his open eyes and a smear of light caught there, thinning and disappearing. The wood of the floor eased his fluids away, splinter by splinter, spreading them thin to make it easier for the air to take them, and after a time his eyes no longer reflected the light. Rafters sprinkled dust. The roof adjusted a shingle and the door creaked open to allow in enough wind to disperse the shards of hair and rotted cloth. And then only the bones remained, sturdy and hard. And so the man became better company for the hut that held him, his skull a home for small scuttling creatures.

Time, for the hut, was measured in tiny shifts of shingle against shingle, the miniscule release of rusted metal as a creaking nail eased from the split wood of a rafter, the exquisite tickle of a termite nibbling through a beam. Fine rain gathered and dripped through a hole in the roof, and there was a tiny moist explosion. Damp crept upwards, fungus feasted on rot and every moment the hut yearned the tiniest fraction of an angle closer to the man. In its own time, it would fall at last onto the bones, and the hut and the man would mingle and return to the earth together.

After Maeve reported her discovery, gloved officials came to inspect the bones, and took them from their place on the hut's floor to a steel-and-white laboratory. The city was closer than it used to be, but still distant. The remains were found to be a male, aged about sixty, identity unknown. Death not suspicious. Speculation and discussion filled half-pages of Sunday newspapers but did not hold people's attention. The man was buried in a bald bland cemetery, the earth above him flat and the grass trimmed neat. A metal plaque with raised words failed to box his story into four straight sides.

The Old Hermit's Hut became a popular attraction, an easy diversion off the new trail. It was discreetly reinforced at its weaker points to ensure it remained upright. Despite the signs and bars and a padlock across the door, people found ways in, to touch things and move them, to leave a dusty footprint in the middle of the stain in the corner, to write words on its walls which had to be removed with caustic fluids. The place was rumoured to be haunted, of course, an irresistible challenge, and in the night there would be pale moving figures, and whispers and shrieks and laughter.

Finally, it was enclosed in a chain link fence and a strongly worded sign, and people passed by and stared and shrugged and walked on. And the hut, caged, was frozen, straining towards the stain that was all that remained of the man, never permitted to fall.

Years passed. The Park Ranger was now the Senior Manager, Strategic Planning and Resources, working on the fifteenth floor of an air-conditioned government building caught in a rigid grid of streets. Each stage of life had drawn her closer to the centre of the city until there was nowhere to go but upwards. She escaped when she could, but often had to work weekends on funding applications and employment agreements and recruitment decisions. Most days she went early to the office, to have at least a little quiet time. The pale gold dawn through the windows was diffused by pollution and announced nothing more than the start of another working week. After her last promotion she put a deposit on a tiny, dim apartment. Her parents were proud.

One Monday morning, an email at the top of her inbox read: *Hermit's Hut Otways National Park: Report.* Maeve had given little conscious thought to the hut over the years, but was now snapped back to the moment before she discovered it. Stillness, smell of damp earth, the mournful cry of black cockatoos as the light faded. An option to turn away, not taken.

She clicked. The report said the upkeep on the hut was expensive, the benefits of maintaining it *in situ* questionable. It should be preserved, of course, but the recommendation was to dismantle it plank by plank and rebuild it at the Museum, safely behind glass 'for everyone to enjoy.' Perhaps an interactive element to the display, lights and buttons, a quiz. A dummy model of the old hermit.

She softly tapped the mouse. The elevator opened, her colleagues streamed in. A ripple of chimes and a flicker of lights as computers started up, low level chatter. More emails, a reminder there was a Teams meeting at nine. She filed the PDF into her already overloaded 'To Be Attended To' electronic folder. Told herself there were more urgent priorities.

Maeve began to wake each morning in a panicky sweat, from dreams she could not recall. The number of things left undone that needed to be done, and decisions taken that perhaps should have been other decisions, was too great to ponder. Anything might be responsible for this sense of dismay that now never quite left her.

In the office she stood at her high window looking out at the city and ran her hand through her short hair, threaded with grey. Among the morning's emails was the latest passive-aggressive reminder requesting a decision on the hut. She could not see the edges of the city, felt vertigo, turned and sat at her desk.

Approve Stage One, she typed. *No other works without my authorization.*

The pack on her back was comfortable, an old friend. With each step, tension trickled down her body, through her soles and out into the neutralising mud. Clouds gathered overhead, low and threatening, but Maeve trudged on, slowly. Her legs were not what they had been.

The earth around the hut was somewhat scarred, and there was damage to the structure where the braces had been removed, as per her instruction. Otherwise it looked much the same as when she first saw it. Inside, she shrugged off her big hiking pack, rolled out her sleeping bag, constructed her camp stove. A few tea bags and tins, a mug and bowl and spoon. The blessings of minimal objects. Finally, carefully, she pulled forth a rattling sack.

'Home,' she said.

Her arms were soft from too much desk work and still tired from her efforts to retrieve the bones, but the hole did not have to be deep. The storm broke as she dug and the hut, though aged and weary, protected her as well as it could. At last she patted the earth flat. She washed her hands in water she had taken from the creek. In the driest corner she ate her beans and bread, listening to the sound of rain on wood. The river would be rising. Tomorrow, she would walk to the waterfall.

Too Much and Not Enough

Kathryn Goldie

Lauren brushes her hair, mouth moving as she counts. She sneaks a look at the clock by the mirror: almost time. She beams—and loses her place. She starts again, from 80, then stops at 100, and pulls her hair into a ponytail that sits a little off-centre.

She draws a thin doona over her bed and twists a pink backpack over her shoulders. She surveys her tidy bedroom from the doorway, then creeps out, closing the door behind her.

The lounge room is chaos. Scarves and magazines threaten to slide from the coffee table. Empty premix bottles cluster on the floor, in thrall to the open gin bottle above them.

Lauren studies her mother. All knotted hair and smudged eyeliner, Tamara is crashed out on the worn couch, a lipstick-smeared glass by her hand. Lauren gently touches Tamara's bare shoulder.

Her mother groans and pushes Lauren's hand away.

Lauren bites her lip and tiptoes into the kitchen.

Breakfast is a silent dance. Lauren moves from fruit bowl to cupboard to fridge: banana, bowl, Coco Pops, milk. She sniffs the milk and scrunches up her face. She looks at the sink and back to the fridge, weighing her decision carefully. She returns the bottle to the fridge door. She holds her breath as she tilts the box of Coco Pops. None come out, so she changes the angle and shakes the box. Cereal cascades over the bowl and onto the floor.

Lauren freezes.

Her mother grunts, swears, from the lounge room. She turns her face into the back of the couch as Lauren scoots past.

On the porch, Lauren stabs the banana into the dry cereal, encrusting it with crunchy chocolate. When it's gone, she scoops the Coco Pops up with her fingers. She looks up at the sound of every approaching car.

When her father's ute appears, a smile splits her face and she races to him.

'How's my princess?' Scott says, scooping her into a bear hug.

'I'm seven tomorrow!' she shouts.

He steps back, open-mouthed. He scratches his head and frowns. 'What? I didn't realise.'

She watches him carefully. When he stops pretending, she beams.

He winks at her. 'Guess we'd better go to the show, then!'

She jumps with happiness, claps her sticky hands.

Scott lifts Lauren into the passenger seat. As he waits for her to fasten her seatbelt, he clocks the half-dead garden and overgrown lawn. He says nothing, but revs the engine extra hard before they drive off.

Town is a few shops in the rear-vision mirror. Scott drives further, to the big smoke. All down the highway, Lauren squirms with excitement. Scott can't stop grinning under her adoring gaze.

'Then Mrs Koustas said Jayden's drawing was wrong cos dogs have four legs,' Lauren chatters, voice rising as her punchline draws closer. 'But she didn't know that Grover only has three legs because Jayden's dad ran him over in the tractor!'

She laughs a breathless laugh, twists her body against the seat.

'Silly Mrs Koustas. Even I know that!' Scott chuckles.

He flicks a glance from the highway to his laughing daughter and keeps his tone light. 'How's your mum? What's the plan for your birthday?'

Lauren stops laughing. For the first time, she turns away from Scott and stares determinedly at the flat, green paddocks out her window. She takes her time bringing her gaze back to her father.

'Grover can't work on the farm anymore, but he barks a lot.'

Scott nods slowly. 'Right.'

Lauren is wary. She looks straight ahead at the grey road and dirty trucks in front of them.

Scott clears his throat and regains his light tone. 'Got one for you: knock, knock.'

She brightens. 'Who's there?'

'Oliver.'

'Oliver who?'

'Oliver sudden my dog started barking!' He glances at her. 'Get it?'

Lauren hesitates. Then she groans and shakes her head, covering her ears.

They both laugh.

The Royal Show is colour and noise and aroma. It's everything, all together, all at once. It's her Dagwood dog, too hot to eat and too heavy to hold, fallen in the dirt, and it's the giant pink fairy floss her dad buys to cheer her up. It's too much and not enough.

Lauren holds Scott's hand tight, lets it go to spin in circles, and grabs it again. He buys her a princess showbag full of shiny silver and pink treasures. She plucks out a sparkly tiara and puts it on.

'Your humble servant,' he says, bowing deeply before her.

Lauren giggles and skips in delight.

She spins with her dad in a giant teacup. She studies the rise and fall of the roller coaster and chooses the super slide instead, holding her tiara firmly in place for the whole ride.

Lauren and Scott grow into towering giants in the dark hall of mirrors. She laughs breathlessly as they stomp and dance with impossibly long limbs. But when the mirrors squash them to half their height and stretch them to double their width, tears pop into her eyes. As Scott carries her out, holding her close, Lauren pulls her tiara down over her eyes. She squints through the silver and pink plastic to make everything sparkle and shine.

In the fresh air of the ring, where everything returns to normal size, they watch pigs run races in the dirt. One after the other, three pigs trot along a plank and drop into a little pool. Lauren frowns and shakes her head. 'It says diving pigs. They're just jumping!'

Each mouthful of the giant fairy floss melts on her tongue and leaves a sugary smear on her cheek, like errant lipstick. She pushes the treat at Scott when they reach the petting zoo. He holds it patiently, with her growing haul of showbags safely at his feet. Lauren weaves past the rabbits, eyes the goats dubiously, scatters the cheeping chicks and makes a beeline for a tiny black lamb half-asleep in the corner. She pulls it onto her lap, crooning and gently stroking its head.

The game arcade is loud and wild, an alley of hot dirt with too many yelling boys. But Lauren is brave enough to lead Scott to her favourite—the clowns—and to stand her ground as she tosses Ping-Pong balls at their open mouths. The light plastic sails past, bounces off a red nose, never hits the target.

Lauren is mesmerised when her dad bends low and offers deft, gentle throws. Her eyes are as big and unblinking as the clowns' when Scott wins and tells her to choose a prize. She considers carefully, then points. The stall holder whistles through his teeth and gets a ladder.

Scott carries the enormous pink bear everywhere, keeping it out of the dirt and away from kids' ice creams. He ignores the smirks of smaller men and teenage boys, and the envy of dozens of little girls. He wedges the bear into their cabin on the ferris wheel. 'So he doesn't miss out,' he grins.

Lauren nestles into Scott as the bear smiles at her. They arc upward, soaring away from the colour and the noise and the heat below.

Night has fallen when they return. Lauren shivers a little as they stand on the porch, waiting for Tamara to open the door. TV noise blares louder when the door finally swings open.

She's not happy to see them.

Scott hesitates, then hugs and kisses Lauren goodnight. 'Happy birthday, sweetie,' he whispers. She beams and drags the pink bear over the threshold and through the mess of the lounge room. She waves at Scott and closes her bedroom door behind her.

She can hear them argue without even pressing her ear to the door.

'How am I supposed to leave her here when you're like this?'

'What do you care? You don't live here anymore.'

'I'm thinking about the kid. Are you?'

Lauren props the bear up on her bed. She unpacks her pink backback, full of showbag treasures: lollies, crayons, stickers, figurines, glitter. She sorts them into neat piles.

'What did she say to you?'

A deep guffaw. 'Didn't have to say anything. Look at the place!' Glass clinks, rolls across the lino, hits something, clinks again.

'Well, if you care so much, you take her.'

Lauren freezes. She holds her breath and listens hard to the silence.

'You know it's not that easy...'

'Yeah, course not,' her mother jeers. 'Not as easy as one day a year.'

Lauren's mouth puckers. She breathes out. As she looks at the treasures on the bed, her eyes become slits.

She topples the piles. Pushes everything onto the floor. Glares at the jumbled plastic. She scoops everything up and dumps it in the back of the wardrobe with the shiny pink and silver treasures from last year's birthday. And the one before that.

'So, what about tomorrow?' Scott asks.

'What about it?'

Lauren shoves the pink bear so hard it tumbles off the bed and lands on its smiling face.

'You having a party for her?'

She pulls on her pyjama top, dislodging her tiara. She flings it onto the dressing table and looks in the mirror at her flushed face.

'Why? You gonna be here?'

The front door slams. The voices stop, but not the TV. There's a hissed string of curses, and then the couch springs creak.

Lauren scrambles over her bed to the window and yanks her blind up, peering into the dark street as the red tail lights of Scott's ute blink on. She mouths a goodbye and swallows a smile as the car pulls away. She watches the silent street until the lights have disappeared, then draws the blind.

In front of the mirror, she picks up the tiara. She rights the unicorn figurine it knocked over, and the mermaid next to it, and whispers an apology to them. She takes a deep breath and holds the tiara over her eyes, squinting as hard as she can so that her world sparkles pink and silver once more. She smooths her hair and slides the tiara on. Finally, Lauren picks up the bear and hauls it into bed with her, under the sheets. She settles herself in its soft pink arms, dabs her eyes with its paw and turns out the light.

Lost at Sea

Martin Watson

Taking down two cups from the cupboard, Thomas turned and placed them neatly on the table, in their saucers, for the last time. He paused then, at the kitchen window, to look down the garden, past the lawn and neat bordered beds, to the vegetable patch—a very productive patchwork of soil which had done unfailingly well over the years, under his practised hands.

His train of thought temporarily dislocated. He moved to the kitchen door and tilted his head meaning to call upstairs, then paused, closed his mouth in the silence, and returned to the kitchen sink to fill the kettle.

Breakfast was then eaten with a sense of purpose, and the plates were washed and put away, so that all was ship-shape and fit for inspection. Thomas was an old salt. As a young man, he had been almost too young to be out there on the waves, in the convoys, but old enough to fool the merchant navy recruiters who had a habit of turning a blind eye when warm bodies were needed. Served King and Country for five years, then jumped ship and wed at twenty. Married for sixty years.

After the war, Thomas had nightmares that were nearly always the same. He was flapping like a gull in the freezing sea, coated in oil as heavy as molasses, and 'going down for the third time', as they used to say. He had seen many men lost that way, watching in horror from the ship's rail as torpedo-stricken ships frothed, hissed and groaned, before giving in to the suck of the sea and disappearing forever, to unmeasured depths. He would awake gasping, in his own sea-salt sweat, crying for the close call, and for those who never came back up. She would wake and watch him, knowing where he had been, but not how he had survived those times.

She learned and, after the first three panicked occasions, they never again spoke about it in the warm benign light of another morning. She had her own nightmares: that she would remain childless. That he would

144

leave her. That he would stop caring. But only one of these proved true, and they accepted life as a childless couple.

Two peas in a pod, Yin and Yang, as close in their pairing as the tick and tock of an old mantlepiece clock, for sixty years.

Thomas walked through the house, closed windows and locked doors, then chose a jacket and cap and headed for the front door, pausing to bend with a groan and pick up his canvas rucksack. He had used it almost to the point of disintegration, hiking through hills, camping in woods and, more recently, for carrying things to the local hospital. He realised that the rucksack had no beginning. He couldn't remember where it came from, except that he had used it on their honeymoon, when times were simpler and a walking holiday was still an acceptable thing to do.

He hefted the bag and realised that there was something in it. Momentarily puzzled, then painfully resigned, he opened the rucksack and took the books, reading glasses and framed photograph out. At a loss, he first put them all on the hall table, but then stood the frame up, put the books on a shelf and, after dithering, slid her glasses into a drawer. He paused one last time to look into her eyes, and into his own, as they both smiled out of the picture at him sixty years ago on their wedding day.

The front door closed with its familiar seismic thud, the chain rattling against the back. Thomas turned the key in the lock and slipped the keys into his pocket, then paused, took them out and, lifting a corner of the doormat, slid them under it, leaving a rather obvious bump.

She had always told him that people who left their keys in obvious spots got burgled. Sixty years ago, he reflected, that didn't happen. People would leave their doors open and go out for the day. They had done the same, but as years went by, they became cautious, especially her, and the door was locked whenever they were going somewhere, even if it was only to the local shop.

Nothing had gone awry in their simple lives; they were content to be together always. People smiled when they saw Thomas holding hands with his wife, whilst both chatted animatedly as though they were young lovers. His years at sea had knocked the wanderlust from him and she was a warm soul, who liked nothing more than running a tidy home and making jams and pies from the fruit of his labours in the garden.

On many evenings past, as a warm golden glow suffused their small cottage garden, bringing a luminous quality to all that it touched, they would sit on a rustic bench with their backs against the sun-warmed wall of their cottage and simply revel in being.

But one day the pain came to her. Thomas heard an intake of breath as she rose from her chair, and looked up from his book with a quizzical expression. She turned a grimace into a smile and carried on. As the weeks went by, however, the pain in her back worsened from needles to knives, with an accompanying dull weight in the centre of her being.

She knew it was wrong. She knew her ageing body and its complaints. But never before this—this draining pain which woke her in the early hours, so that she would lie awake and watch Thomas drowning night after night, with his twitching eyelids, flailing arms and, finally, the sweat-soaked awakening as he escaped into consciousness again.

Then she could not bear the aches, or hide the pain any longer. She and Thomas went hand in-hand to a doctor. Neither of them knew him, as they had never had to trouble the local surgery with their minor ailments, living through times when traditional cures were better than a whole lot of pills and tablets, with all that they cost.

The doctor sent her for x-rays, then to a specialist who told them both as they sat forward nervously on uncomfortable chairs, that it was cancer. It was cancer in her spine, which had spread throughout her internal organs, and meant that there was nothing that could be done, and that she had a matter of weeks left. All they could do, he said, was make her comfortable and ensure that her last weeks were as pain-free as they could be.

Shocked beyond words, they went home to face the coming weeks together. It wasn't long, though, before she'd had to move into the hospital, her pain increasing to a point where even strong drugs did little to alleviate the agony. Thomas came in every morning, as soon as he was allowed, and stayed until nightfall, taking only short breaks from her bedside, whilst she lay and slept or tried to smile at him through the pain. Her books and glasses lay untouched on the bedside cabinet.

The nurses would whisper to each other about the love and dedication of the elderly couple as Thomas held her hand, leaning forward and staring intently at her, whilst she slept, winced and occasionally groaned, with her illness worsening and taking an ever-tighter grip.

On a Thursday morning in June, Thomas had risen early to walk to the hospital. When he arrived, a senior nurse was waiting for him. Take

146

a seat, she had said. They had tried to call, they wanted to contact him as soon as possible, as his wife's condition had worsened overnight, she said. They were so sorry, the nurse said, but his wife had passed away thirty minutes ago.

He sat and held her hand for the last time. It was still warm and her face looked serene, as the pain had slipped away with her final breath. Totally lost, he was handed her books and glasses, which he put in his rucksack.

They would make arrangements, they told him, and that he needn't worry as the funeral director would be in touch.

When you are old, and you have no children and your friends have died, a funeral becomes a small affair. Her name was Esme. He always called her Essy, but the vicar didn't know that and the service was all the more impersonal for it.

Leaving their house behind, Thomas made his way down to the shoreline, where the shingle beach sat close to the fishing harbour, and where the boats and ferries set out to sea. He and Essy had often brought sandwiches and tea down here, to feel the breeze and to watch the boats and the gulls.

He sat on the pebbles for half an hour or so, looking out towards the islands where the ferries plied their routes. As he did so, he ran the soft, sun-warm, rounded stones between his fingers, listening to them clatter softly as they fell into his rucksack, some of them making a gentle click as they hit the small ceramic urn which lay at the bottom.

Daylight faded and the last ferry was preparing to leave for its final round trip of the day, to return well after dark. Thomas paid for a ticket and boarded with a knot in his stomach. He had not been on a boat since his wartime experience, and had never intended to do so again. He still knew the sea though, and he knew the islands offshore, the channels that ran between them and the rips and tides that shaped the rocky coastline.

He took a seat outside, at the stern of the almost empty ferry, whilst the other passengers chose to sit inside out of the breeze which, with the lowering of the sun in a clear blue, vaulting sky, had some bite to it. Thomas didn't mind though; this weather was as nothing compared to the convoys, with their freezing gale force winds, stinging spray and ice on the decks.

With a blast of its horn, the ferry moved away from the quay and out towards the furthest island, three miles offshore. As it left the lee of the harbour in the calm of evening, the swell rose a little and pitched the vessel gently too and fro. Thomas felt once more the thrum and   pulse of a diesel engine beneath his feet and had to quell a moment of anxiety as he was transported back once more to the thud of a torpedo's explosion and the ensuing panic which saw his ship slide beneath the waves, leaving him and his shipmates in the freezing water.

In the gloaming now, the sun still lit the sky from below the horizon, whilst to the east, darkness started to encroach. The ferry was halfway to its first stop, a mile and a half offshore. It was, Thomas knew, in the middle of a channel that sunk to eighty fathoms below the keel. He went to the rail and looked at the sea, fizzing and spilling brightly along the side of the hull but dark and brooding a little further off. He was afraid now, shivering through fear rather than the cold, but knowing that it would soon be gone.

Sitting back down on his bench at the stern of the ferry, he tightened the straps on the trusty rucksack across his shoulders. Then, as easily as an eighty-year-old-man carrying a weight is able to, he pushed himself to sit on the top of the bench, with his back to the sea. He raised his eyes to the sky, where he saw the first stars of evening appear over his head. Gently tilting further back, he let the momentum of the ferry rock him backwards into the water with only a small, barely noticeable splash, surrendering at last with Essy to the sea he had fought for so long.

Girl

Keren Heenan

The girl is not so sure now. She'd been in such a state of excitement in this vast new world of the city: the hotel room with all its shiny surfaces and plump bedcovers; buildings so tall she strained her neck looking up at them; the restaurant with its dance floor and live band; waiters who said, *would you like a drink madam?* and didn't treat her and her friend like they were seventeen. The handsome man with the dark hair looking at her across the room.

At first the attention, right there under the watchful eye of her aunt, had made her feel as if she had a secret, one so big she could burst. But then he'd undone her bra, right there on the dance floor. While she was holding onto his arms in the way she thought you had to for a waltz. While she was looking about wondering if her friend was envious, if anyone else was looking, maybe thinking, *I wish that was me, young and pretty and dancing with an older handsome man.*

Now she is stricken with unease and she notices the man's yellow teeth, his tobacco breath, and the way his hand has slipped from her waist down to her hip, his fingers stretching towards her bottom. She takes his arm and lifts it to her waist again. Sees her aunt watching as he steers her firmly through the couples on the dance floor, closer to the hallway leading to the toilets. The sign, *Restrooms*, in fancy lettering would, under normal circumstances, makes her laugh. What does one do in a *Restroom*? Lie around? She wants to be laughing at this with her friend, but her friend is sitting, turned away from the girl with a look on her face that says, *I wish that was me on the dance floor.*

She wants the music to stop, wants to rush back to her friend, pull her away to the toilets so they can laugh together at the man's hands, his teeth and the way he looked at her, like he was about to huff and puff and blow her away.

The girl and her friend had been pleased to be escorted to the city by the youngish, daring and do-as-she-pleases aunt. They'd managed to contain their excitement in front of their parents but whooped and hugged each other later when they were alone. Neither of their parents could make the trip; too busy, and they had no interest in spending a couple of days in the city. The girl had hounded her aunt for an alcoholic drink as soon as they arrived at the restaurant. After much begging, her aunt had finally given in—wine with soda water. The girl was impressed with the elegance of it in a proper wine glass. Not so pleased with the taste which she thought was a little like the smell of cat's piss. But her friend was nodding, saying it was 'ni-ice,' and she nodded too, gulped a large mouthful in one swallow so she didn't have to taste it.

When she'd seen the tall man with the black hair and moustache looking at her, she'd pretended not to notice. Sipped her drink, holding on to the stem of the glass, pressing her throat closed to stop from pulling a face at the taste. She'd crossed her legs and sat up straight, recrossed her legs and looked around at the people, the paintings on the wall, the band. Eventually he came right over to the table, leant down and said to her, 'May I have the pleasure of this dance?', and she'd wanted to laugh along with her friend, who'd looked across the table at her with her mouth open and eyebrows raised. But she wasn't laughing. She'd closed her mouth and looked away, and the girl stood up. The man held out his hand and she took it, smoothed her skirt down with her other hand.

In her mind's eye, she saw so many people watching: *how lucky, look at her, so pretty, her skirt such a lovely red, so sophisticated with her wine, and now she's dancing with the most handsome man in the room.* She'd twirled around in his arms as he gazed down at her and she tried not to notice him looking down the front of her shirt. He said something to her but she couldn't hear over the music and she smiled and glanced away. Then his hand had inched its way up from her waist to between her shoulder blades and he'd undone her bra.

Now, she tries to propel him back through the twirling couples, back to the side where her aunt and friend are sitting. But he resists her efforts, looking down at her with a smile that freezes her daydream of sophistication and envy. She braces her arms against her sides, trying to hold the bra in place, but he keeps lifting her arms higher and she feels the loose bra floating around her breasts. She stiffens as his gaze darts down the front of her shirt again and she looks away, through the dancers to her aunt who is straining to see across the crowded dance floor from her seat at the table. Her friend's fingers drum on the tabletop and her face is turned away as if she is studying the artwork on the wall.

After what feels like an eternity of squirming and pulling away, the music stops and the girl darts away from him, before he can speak to her or walk her back to the table. She gives a quick smile to her aunt, one that says, *I know, don't say anything*, then pulls her friend's hand. 'Come to the loo with me.'

The toilets are empty, much to her relief, and she unleashes her story to her friend who is aghast and helps do her bra hook up through her shirt, frowning then sighing in relief that it hadn't been her on the dance floor in his creepy arms. The girl rushes in to the toilet cubicle, sits and sees that she has her period, calls out, 'Nooo! Do you have a tampon?'

Her friend gasps and calls back, 'No, I don't. Oh no!' The girl uses wads of toilet paper and places it inside her undies. She flushes the toilet, feeling damp and uncomfortable now.

'Is it on my skirt?' She turns around for her friend to see, her hand brushing the back of her skirt.

'No, you're fine. At least your skirt is red though.'

They study their faces in the mirror, touch their hair, pushing and pulling it into place. A woman walks in and glances at them and they leave, the door banging behind them. On their way back to the table the girl sees the man over in a corner talking to a group of people. She quickly looks away.

Back at the table they sit and the girl picks up her wine glass, puts it to her lips then places it on the table again. Her friend has finished her drink but the girl has no interest in the wine anymore. She looks around to the corner where she'd last seen the man. He is still there, his hand on the back of a chair, leaning down talking to a woman. The woman suddenly pushes her chair back and walks towards the toilets. The man straightens up and turns to look around the room. The girl spins away, leans in to her friend to speak to her.

'Come on, you two,' her aunt says, standing and putting her jacket on. 'We've got an early start tomorrow. We'd better get to bed.'

Tomorrow is enrolment day. The girl had almost forgotten with all the fizz and ferment of the day: the train, the city, the shopping, the hotel, the restaurant, and then the man. She and her friend have chosen the same subjects; they'll be in all the same lectures, hopefully the same tutorials too.

They'll be living on campus, so no parents or older sisters to nag, *don't eat that, don't do that, don't say that, don't wear that.* Her eighteenth birthday is coming up and her father has even promised her a car. The world is vast and new and everything glitters—even the memory of a creepy man's hands on her. Now that he's not so close.

The hotel has that smell like the carpet is new, or the curtains, or it's all just been mopped and wiped and polished. Everything is beige and white. The girl and her friend go to their room while the girl's aunt has a 'nightcap', a whiskey from the minibar. The girl takes a tampon and goes to the toilet, flushing the wads of toilet paper away. Back in the room she falls onto her bed, arms flung out. 'Today has been so-ooo good. Apart from creepy bra man, and my bloody period, I can do without that right now,' she says. Her friend laughs, her eyes wide, and she sits on her bed and bounces up and down. They clean their teeth and change into pyjamas.

The girl stands at the window a while, looking down over the street where couples walk arm in arm, chattering, laughing. She watches the way the girls lean in, heads resting on a shoulder or arm. How steadily they walk in heels, how easy the quiet comfort of their man's arm. Lights shine from bars and restaurants and bursts of music punctuate the throb of the city.

The girl and her friend both fall into bed, pull the covers up and talk and laugh until the girl's aunt calls out, 'Girls, time for sleep,' and they giggle in a hushed way and whisper goodnights and sleep wells, then close weary eyes.

Sometime during the night the girl wakes to the noise of shouting out in the street, swearing and rough sounds that aren't words, not full words anyway. She looks over to her friend's bed, the top of her head just visible under the cover, and she hears her steady breath in the gaps between the noises outside. She puts one hand between her legs and checks for any leaks or dampness, but it's all fine. She gets up and goes to the window.

Under a street light below, a man is slumped against the hotel wall, a bottle wrapped in a brown paper bag beside him. He blusters and roars as if fending off an attacker, flings out an arm and knocks the bottle over. The girl looks up and down the street. Almost empty apart from one man walking by, hands in pockets, head down. Most of the pulsing bright lights from before and the buzz of sound have gone. The street is dark apart from the lamps here and there along its length. She looks back to the man against the wall, crabbing his arms and legs like he's trying to get up, a beetle on its back. He gives in and slides further down the wall, a final 'argh' flung out to the empty street.

The girl watches him, his head slumped on his chest, arms useless at his sides. A dark stain spreads from between his splayed legs, and a rivulet seeps toward the gutter. She steps back from the window, something heavy in her chest. Something just as big as the glittering world had been when she was twirling in the arms of the man, before he became *creepy man*. Then the sour taste of the wine rises up and grips her throat, and she feels sick and sad and yanks the curtains closed. Stumbles back to bed, pulls up the cover and holds it tight under her chin. She stares into the half dark, this new ugliness crashing and jangling around her.

My Cousin Has Bought a Metal Detector

Catherine Moffat

My cousin has bought a metal detector. He wants to dig up our grandfather. Following my uncle's last long, slow fall down the front steps of the Queenslander, the house is to be sold. The broken railing has been repaired, the jasmine and frangipani chopped back, the deck rubbed with oil. The untethered awning that bangs like an angry fist on the kitchen window will be removed.

I help Ryan carry heavy boxes from under the house. They're rotten, splitting at the sides and ripe with mottled mould. All that is left to do is clear this under-house cave, dank with earth smell, animal must and the scent of gardenia bushes grown so large they block the light. And to find my grandfather, of course.

'I think I can remember the spot,' Ryan says. 'I was fourteen. A surly, lazy, teenager. It was summer. I didn't bother to dig too deep.' He has a couple of surly teenagers himself. One is slowly hosing down the path in the front garden while simultaneously watching YouTube on his phone.

The house auction is on Saturday and the metal detector is coming from eBay. It's unlikely it will arrive in time. If it doesn't, the next chance we have to get to the yard will be more than six weeks away. Ryan works FIFO at Mount Isa and will be back on rotation. There's a strong chance the house will be sold by then, and our grandfather with it.

Me, I'm not fussed. In a sense our grandfather has always been buried, hidden, under layers of mystery. Don't ask. Don't tell. As kids we were told he was dead.

Wished dead, perhaps. But not. Not then.

This old house is the one Ryan grew up in. A house of women. His mother, our grandmother and 'Auntie Rae'—not a real aunt, but someone my grandmother had befriended and taken in. We knew, somehow without

154

being told, that Rae had had a hard life, with unfortunate relationships, as had Grandma. Ryan was at the centre of this group—the only child, a boy, fussed over and spoilt. My sister, Annie, and I called him the Sun King.

Like Ryan, my uncle worked in the mines and spent weeks, sometimes months, away from home, in New Guinea, in Mount Isa, Kalgoorlie, wherever the job took him. When he was home, he sat out in the sun or dozed in the shade with a newspaper or a book, drifting, and making no visible contribution to the conversation or life of the house.

Ryan and I drink beer and lie back on mattresses on the covered verandah where we slept whenever I stayed as a kid. The house has been emptied. Tomorrow we will sling the watermarked mattresses into the skip and that will be that. The place is a shell of the former home. A ghost house, waiting to be rewritten with new memories, a new family.

'I met him, our grandfather, once,' Ryan says. It's an old story, but I let it unravel with the beers, with the warmth of the evening. His mother had a sick friend she visited every week. A Mrs McGillicuddy. The clue was in the dodgy name, but no one ever took any notice. My aunt was self-contained, quiet. Competent without appearing to be. The sort who does good by stealth. And she was doing good then, visiting her father in the hostel where he lived without telling her mother or her family.

One day after school, Ryan answered the phone. The old house telephone that still stood on a tiny table in the hallway. The call was from the hostel. Could he give his mother a message? His grandfather was creating havoc with the nurses, chasing them around the ward. Could she come in and help quieten him down? Ryan got the address of the place, jumped on his bike and started peddling.

'When I walked in, I knew at once which one was him,' Ryan says. 'He looked just like your dad.'

I wonder for the first time if this is true, or just part of the family myth that has arisen, the stories we tell ourselves. In this narrative I am 'just like my father', who is 'like his father', meaning wild, impulsive, liable to get into trouble, whereas Ryan and my sister Annie are 'like my aunt', supposedly quiet, good children.

Neither is true. Every piece of trouble I have gotten into in my life has been led by either Ryan or Annie. I can't help thinking that Ryan is leading me into another disaster now. And, as in the past, somehow I will be the one left with the blame.

People made slips about the truth, of course, when we were children. There were hints our grandfather wasn't dead. One of Dad's cousins told Annie she'd seen our grandfather. There was the old man selling the *Big Issue* on a street corner in Brisbane that Dad used to buy a paper from every time we came to visit Grandma. We thought he just called everyone 'son'. They'd stand chatting for a moment, Dad would pass over some money, then we'd move on.

I cannot imagine from the stories that have filtered down about our grandfather that this man was ever like my cynical, melancholic, self-effacing father. My grandfather was violent, we knew. Much later, when he was really dead, and my aunt was dying, stories had come out. The drunken rages he took out on my father. The frequent benders. The time he held the axe to Grandma's throat and asked my six-year-old aunt why he shouldn't cut it. The bewildering changes of temperament and enthusiasms. Christian to Communist to a different brand of Christianity to something else again. His long, unexplained disappearances.

And then there were the women. When he left for the war in New Guinea my grandmother was already pregnant with my father. A shot-gun wedding, by Annie's calculations. When Grandma went to meet him at the end of the war, proudly holding the hand of his toddler son, she found another woman there to meet him too. There was a third woman as well. When Ryan got our grandfather's war service record, it contained a copy of a letter from his commanding officer to a father who had been enquiring 'on behalf of his daughter' whether my grandfather was a married man. This was a pattern that continued.

It's here that I think he must have been more like Ryan. Someone so full of charm, so secure in himself, that he could talk people into doing things against their better judgement. Ryan could always do it to me, which is why I found myself, six weeks after the house had been sold, crouching in the dark beside him while he waved a metal detector around the yard.

Annie had wanted to come with us but she was seven months pregnant, so we'd restricted her to driving the get-away-car. She could have had my place if she wanted, but Ryan said he needed someone to help him with the digging.

'Stop being so gutless,' he said. 'The place is empty. They haven't moved in.'

There were no lights on in the house, but a child's tricycle on the path

156

and two sets of thongs near the back steps seemed to put the lie to his claim.

'Just get a move on,' I said.

We were searching for the metal tin that contained our grandfather's ashes. But we may as well have been looking for a body. My aunt had brought his remains home one day after he died, and then panicked because she didn't want her mother to find them. She thrust the tin at Ryan and told him to bury it.

'It was somewhere near the apple tree, I think,' he says.

'You think? I thought you knew.'

'Yeah, sure I do. Somewhere here.' I can't see his face clearly in the dark but I know he's smiling his big cheese-eating grin.

We search for an hour or so, but it feels like much longer. Every beep from the stupid machine, every sound nearby making me more nervous. We find nothing. A bottle cap, an old metal toy car that Ryan holds up with an excited, 'Hey remember playing with this?'

I don't and I don't care. Neither do I care about finding my grandfather. He can rest in peace, or the opposite of peace, for all I care. I wonder if it actually matters to Ryan or if this is just another one of his adventures. And what was Ryan intending to do with the ashes if he did find them? Prop them up next to the television? Scatter them near our grandmother who said she never wanted to see him again?

What difference does it make to anything whether we find the ashes or not?

I'm about to tell Ryan I've had enough when I hear what I've been dreading. A light going on in the kitchen of the house and the sound of the back door screen sliding open. The dark shadow of a man standing on the verandah.

Ryan thrusts the metal detector towards me and takes off running down the side of the house to the street where Annie is waiting in the car. I'm left lumbering behind, metal detector in one hand, spade in the other. I may as well have a mask on and a striped shirt and a bag marked 'booty'.

I hear shouting behind me as Ryan vaults the front gate.

I realise suddenly that both spade and metal detector belong to Ryan and heave them over the fence into the yard next door. I don't look back but I imagine things behind me. I'm sure I hear a dog growling.

I think about a family moving to a new house, a new place, trying to do the best by their children. I picture a child hearing noises in the dark, looking out, seeing lights in the garden and next morning finding holes beneath a tree. Conjuring pixies, fairies, buried treasure. Trying to piece together a story from the little it hears, the tiny bits it knows.

I catch the toe of my trainer on the top rail as I jump the gate and faceplant in the dirt on the other side. Fear makes me leap up quickly. The man is shouting louder. Ryan has the back door of the car open but Annie is already driving off. I race after them up the street. Ryan urges me to run faster like someone in one of those American movies jumping a box car on a train. I speed up and dive headlong across the back seat, hitting my chin on Ryan's knee as I fall into his lap.

Ryan and Annie are practically pissing themselves laughing.

'Oh God, you should see your face,' says Ryan.

'Stop, stop,' Annie shrieks. 'I can hardly drive. I'm going to wet myself if I laugh any harder.'

'Did you find him?' Annie finally asks when she and Ryan have calmed down a bit.

'No. The new owners heard us. We'll have to go again tomorrow.' Ryan says.

'Count me out.'

'Don't be such a wuss.'

'You're the one who took off like his arse was on fire,' I say.

'Yeah, well I thought the old fella had come back to life and was right behind me.'

This sets us all off laughing, and I know that tonight will become one of the stories that binds us, a tale that will change in the telling—the run becoming longer and more desperate, the digging deeper, more frantic, my fall more comical. It will become a story passed on to our children, twisting with each retelling, changing, ultimately becoming, like us, forgotten, meaningless.

Superman

Dan Davies

I don't know how old I was. Time doesn't register properly with me anymore. Most people say things like, 'Such and such happened to me when I was five-and-a-half.' I can't do that. I was seven or nine, okay, somewhere in there, probably, and guess what? I came to the realisation that I was Superman. Really, no shit! I was clearly Superman because I had on the outfit. Tight-fitting blue onesie with the red bikini bottom, yellow belt, red cape, big 'S' on my chest — I was thrilled! But then I looked down and noticed I only had one red boot. My left, blue-stockinged leg was bootless!

Once, I had a dream I went to school with no pants on. It was awful.

I knew I needed two boots for authenticity, so I was relieved to see my other red boot lying on the floor nearby. Eagerly pulling it on, I realised it was not an exact match with my right boot, but the difference was negligible. Still, it was in the back of my mind as I assumed the take-off position. I bent my knees and elbows, looked towards the heavens, and thrust myself upwards, shooting my arms into the air as I did so, carelessly disregarding the ceiling and roof above me. But nothing happened. No launch. I tried a couple more times with no result. Something is wrong, and I reckon it's this dodgy left boot.

One time, when I was two or four, Dad took us to see Santa at the shopping centre and I was pretty excited. But his beard was wonky, and he smelled of cigarettes. When he picked me up, I kicked and yelled. Santa is creepy.

In frustration, I pull off the dodgy left boot and throw it on the floor. That's when I see another red boot lying just through the doorway. Ha! Simple mistake: I put the wrong boot on. No wonder I couldn't fly.

Once, Mum locked her keys in the car and me and Dad drove all the way across town with the spare set for her. But when we got there, Dad had brought the wrong keys. Mum called him a 'stupid hairy goat.' We didn't get any dinner that night.

So I pull on this second red boot, confident I've sorted the problem. Up, up and away I go...but still nothing. What the...I look down and examine this second left boot more closely. The colour is perfect, deep red, with yellow-gold trim around the cuff, but whereas my right boot has a small V-cut through the trim at the front, my left one does not.

'Well, that's bloody annoying,' I huff as I scan the room. Luckily, I notice yet another red left boot with yellow-gold trim lying nearby. This must be it, third time lucky. I throw off the wrong left boot and pull on the new one, pretty sure it will work now. Okay, it's a match, except the heel is ever so slightly taller on this one.

My sister had a short boyfriend. He was really nice. He would smile and talk to me, and he once showed me his webbed toes. My sister dumped him and got a new boyfriend, who was a jerk. She knew it too, but she said he was the right height for her.

I'm sure a tiny difference in the heel height won't matter. I'm going outside to test this one.

Alright, I'm going to do this. Once again, I bend my knees and elbows, look towards the heavens, and thrust myself upwards, shooting my arms into the air. Once again, nothing happens. What the bloody hell! I am wasting good flying time here.

One time, Mum waited all day for Dad to remember her birthday, but he forgot. Mum made him sleep in the shed. He got bitten by a spider. He didn't get any powers.

This is getting annoying. I look around in frustration and, to my surprise and relief, I see several more boots spaced at regular intervals, leading to the garden gate. How strange, but it makes sense that one of these will work.

I start trying on more boots.

When I was younger, there were toys in cereal boxes. I became somewhat obsessed with collecting the set, of which there were twelve. It was fun at first, discovering the new ones to add to my set, but I could never complete it. And, as the weeks rolled on, it became a torment, as each new cereal box produced a figurine I already had.

So, I try these boots on and I try to fly, but as before, each boot has a subtle difference. One's redness is flecked with tiny metallic gold speckles. One has the trim and the V-cut, but the cuff is an inch lower. One's toe is just a little too pointed. I'm starting to get annoyed. From the garden gate, I can see a trail of red boots leading off toward a hill along a narrow arc of road. Oh shit!

One by one, I try the left boots on. This is becoming a futile exercise as all the boots differ slightly with some minor variation, but surely one of them must work. Each time I thrust my body skyward in anticipation, I experience disappointment. The initial thrill of suspense is diminishing, being eroded by a creeping tide of apprehension, as I repeatedly fail to leave the ground.

When I was littler, I spent all my money at a sideshow trying to win a silver cap gun. You had to pop balloons with darts. You got three for a dollar. If you popped a balloon, it revealed a ticket corresponding to a prize. I threw twenty-one darts, I popped fifteen balloons, but I never got that cap gun.

The red boot trail stretches out before me. Twenty steps away, then thirty. I forge onward, still resolved to find the right left boot, keen to attain my powers of flight and impress my family.

It will be great when I do find the right left boot. Flying is about as cool as it gets. I'll fly straight home and completely freak out Mum and Dad. My brothers and sister will be so jealous and won't even believe it, but they'll have to, because I will shoot up into the sky and do a quick lap around town.

Not very long ago, so it would be safe to say I was eight, or nine, a brand-new BMX bike was given to me. It was brilliant! Metallic orange with black trim and pads, and big knobbly tyres. It said 'Mongoose' on the frame, and I thought it was the best thing ever. There was a show on TV called 'BMX Bandits', and I'd seen some older kids at the park doing some jumps and stuff. I couldn't wait to be part of that action. I rode down to the park feeling supremely confident. I'd dreamed of this. The older kids saw me and came over straight away. They seemed impressed and wanted to know what I could do. I told them I knew a few tricks. I didn't. They wanted me to show them, and I said I could. I spotted a picnic table and said I could jump off it. They seemed more impressed, and told me to do it. It looked a lot higher once I'd lifted my bike awkwardly on to the table and clambered on, but my audience was encouraging. I thought it would be simple, to just ride off the table and land, but I had no momentum as I tried to peddle and balance. The front wheel just nose-dived, and the bike and I crashed to the ground. I can remember them riding off, laughing hard, as I realised I was in pain, and my bike's handlebars were bent.

Where is this trail of boots leading me? I must have tried on more than fifty red left boots by now. I'm hungry, and I'm getting further away from home. Some of these boots aren't even worth trying on — one is just a dusty red gumboot.

This is tiring. I don't know how long I've been at it, but it feels like it's getting late in the day. The boots have led me to a winding lane, bordered by dry brown grass. The trail sways gradually uphill to a small wooden shack that looks like an endpoint to me. I still have to try all these left boots though, just in case. This is exhausting.

When the ambulance came and took me away, I was freaking out about my bike. I didn't want to leave it there. I didn't want to go. Then I saw my sister with my bike, and my concern shifted to what my parents would say.

I'm at the shack now, more of a shed really. Small and decrepit. I have tried on seventy to ninety red left boots by now, and none of them have enabled me to shoot into the sky. But I feel a buzz of excitement return, as I feel sure that this is what it has all been leading to. The right red left boot must be in here. Finally, I will be Superman and I can get into some proper action.

The sun is settling in the west. There is a soft glow in the air. This is it. I smash open the door of the little shack with a super kick. It crashes against the wall, scattering clouds of dust that dance in the light. There is a little window on the far wall. I peer in as the dust settles and my eyes adjust, heart thumping.

Once in a while, I can't say how often, I go down to the park and think about how to jump off that table. Once, Dad caught me trying to get up there, but my wheelchair was too heavy. He cried and pushed me home. I don't know why he cried. It was my own stupid fault.

But it doesn't matter, because here I am, Superman, the most powerful being in existence, and the goal of my quest must be here. I take a deep breath, and behold, there on the floor of the dusty little shack, rather than the one, perfect, red left boot with yellow-gold V-cut trim that I so desperately want and need, there is a huge pile, as tall as me, of red left boots. I mean hundreds upon hundreds of red left boots.

My dream is over.

Opal
Michael Mueller

He used to fish with his grandfather. He now fished alone.

The boy who fished made his way to the river. The day was green and grey. A warmth, a stickiness, a low wetness. He followed the gravelly path.

Soon the gravel gave way to the green and beyond the green lay the watery brown.

The boy set down his bucket and rod. Next to their log. He moved silently, smoothly. The line was baited, its hook in the water.

Some days, the hook gleamed unbaited in the water. Some days, he would sit and the hook stayed dry. Some days, he arrived but did not stay.

This day moved round him like a quilted breeze. In the distance hummed the traffic on the bridge. Closer, the twitching undergrowth spoke of insects and lizards. Birds occasionally shared their secrets.

The boy was thin-legged, tanned like softened leather by the baking sun. His shirt was yellow, his shorts red, his thongs blue. All primary, all worn, they hung from him with the comfort of shadows. His eyes, brown like polished jarrah, looked over the river and into it. He saw into the nature of it. And in return, it stilled him inside.

The line soon flicked and bobbed in the water. A nibble, a bite. The boy didn't react. No desire in him to pull a creature from its world. The line continued to pull against his finger's inner crease. The fish had hooked itself. It could not break free. He reeled it in, eyes mostly closed, unblinking.

Below the murk came a silvery flash. A bream. The line lifted it out of the water. The bream flailed helplessly, urgently. The boy reached out and soon held its quicksilver flesh in his hand. Glistening and quivering.

He removed the hook from her mouth and gently slid her back into the water, his face like a prayer.

Time passed by and it ran through his fingers like water.

In glimpses, he saw his grandfather. Felt him in his old places. Their log. A cut in the trunk of a ghost gum, the beginning of their names. The soft merging of gravelly dust and river clay. The smell of rain glimmering, the mudlark song echoing.

Today was grandfather's birthday. A weight like a stone held tight to the chest.

Kindly eyes never judging, patient and benign. The roughness of his hand, and the gentleness of his grip. His strength and endurance, and his weathered tenderness.

Moments that could not quite be held could not be let go. Breath, drawn and expelled, left an imprint like the swirls that tip the fingers.

His fingers curled the slender rod, its deep green-black of submerged moss, specked with light inside its all-spine body.

Suddenly, the line flicked so hard it caught him by surprise. The rod near pulled from his hand. His eyes widened.

The pull on the line only intensified. The thin nylon should snap, but it would not. The boy moved to his feet, dragged himself to the log's far side and braced his hold.

He too was caught. To cut the line was risky. A hand from the rod to reach his knife. The tension was intense. One sharp pull and both would be gone. He didn't want to lose the gift. He didn't want to take a life.

He doubted his strength. He possessed a desire that betrayed him. He wanted to leave the creature where it belonged, but he wanted to see it. His mind sought reason; perhaps it didn't belong there. It would be right to make sure. His mind looked into his grandfather's eyes. They remained clear, kind, inscrutable.

He began to reel in the line. The rod arched like a hoop, flicked like a whip. Slowly, the reel turned. The line inched in.

The boy was sweating and the line did not break.

He longed to let go. The pain in his arms unbearable. Sinews near breaking point. But he could not let go.

Suddenly, a flash in the water. Perfect white, pure as lightning. *Close.*

His mind began to colour and swirl. Light-headedness. Minutes that felt like hours. He drained like a punctured pouch, the very essence of himself ebbing out of his body, into his hands, down the spine of the rod and the sinews of the line, and into the water. As he pulled the fish in, his life was drained out. All was wrong. It was happening.

And then the fight dissolved into a moment that would remain in his mind like an insect in amber.

With a rifle-crack, the rod snapped. And the fish flew from the water.

It was impossibly beautiful. It took the light, refracted it and splintered it to rainbows. Every scale, a prismatic flash. It seemed to bend the light around itself, its size a dazzling mystery. It flew through the air like it could fly.

The boy heard a hard snap above him. A twisted branch ripped from the tree above and, before the boy had a chance, it fell upon him.

And all went black, until it became light again.

He finally sat up. He felt his forehead and found dried blood. He looked about him. On either side lay two halves of the fallen limb. The broken ends were crushed, as if by a heavy stone.

He turned his head upwards and saw from where the branch as thick as his waist had fallen. He knew it should have killed him.

He finally, unsteadily rose and looked about. One half of his broken rod poking out of the water. He took a few steps to retrieve it. The broken half in his hand felt light, shimmering in its wetness, now as straight as a sword.

The fish. Where had it gone? In his mind, he could see it clearly, hovering in mid-air like a tamed spirit. He could feel the life of it, radiating outward like a pulse of blood, its colours a trapped kaleidoscope, a living opal. Had it landed back in the water? Impossible. Its trajectory was arching over him.

He looked around behind him. There was no sign of it. No sign it had ever landed. No sign it ever existed. He looked at the tree with its massive, broken limb, and felt a prickling sensation, a low hum from within.

A dizzying flash of colours. He felt himself sink to his knees. He could not tell if the colour was around him or within him.

In moments, it was gone.

Burial of a Dream

Jim Brigginshaw

SEVEN o'clock. And Charlie knocked off at the mine at four. Clara knew he'd be at the Grand Hotel, a drinking hole that was anything but grand. If he couldn't get an argument there, he'd come home and start one with the family.

She had the meal ready hours ago but the two boys had to wait—Charlie said they had to all eat together.

George, nineteen, worked with his dad down the mine and hated every minute of it. He'd wanted to be an architect, but when he was sixteen his father said he had to take a job down below to help with his keep.

The other son, Herbie, sixteen and still at school, dreamed of becoming a professional footballer. Nobody called him Herbie, everyone knew him as Tammy. It was because of his freckles. When the other kids saw *Tam-Tam the Leopard Man* in a sideshow tent covered in gingery blotches, they called their mate Tam-Tam, then shortened it. Soon the Herbie was forgotten and he was known to all as Tammy Meetson, the kid with a footballing dream.

In the kitchen now, Tammy was grumbling about being hungry.

'You'll have to wait,' his mother said. 'You know your father hits the roof if we eat without him.' She heard a car door slam. 'There he is now.'

Charlie Meetson stood swaying in the doorway. Panda rings of coal dust circled his eyes and made him look ridiculous. But nobody was laughing, he was in one of his drunken moods. He waved an arm at the three standing around the table. 'Look at you…like hungry bloody crows. Can't wait to feed your faces.'

He slumped into a chair. The family knew that was the signal they could join him.

Charlie began to eat noisily. He pointed his fork at his youngest son.

'You, Herb.' He never used Tammy, said it was a girl's name. 'Don't you think it's time you earnt a few quid instead of eating your head off and letting me pay for it? Your brother George was down the pit at your age. And I was filling coal long before I was sixteen.'

Tammy knew his father was spoiling for a row. But he decided to take a stand. 'Say the word, Dad, and I'll leave school.'

'Good boy. I'll put in a word for you at the mine.'

Tammy took a deep breath. 'I won't be going down the mine.'

His father's face turned red, a vein pulsated in his forehead. Crockery rattled as he thumped the table with his fist. '*What ... !* The pit's not good enough for you, that it?'

'That's right, the pit's not good enough. I've seen you and George coughing your lungs up—that's what the pit's done for you.'

Charlie Meetson's mouth opened and shut like a fish deprived of oxygen. Words came in a torrent: 'The pit's put food on the table for all of you.' He thumped the table again for emphasis. 'I was providing for this family long before George had the good sense to follow me down below.'

Tammy steeled himself to continue: 'George followed you down the pit because you made him do it. He wanted to be an architect. You ended his ambition.'

Charlie nearly choked. 'Ended his ambition, did I? And what ambition do you have, Mister High and Mighty?'

Here goes, Tammy told himself. 'People say I might make the grade as a professional footballer. Not yet…some day. I want to get a job, salesman or something, where I'll be breathing fresh air. If I go down the pit I'll end up like you—left without enough breath to run across the road.'

His father was dribbling in his anger. '*Salesman!* To think I reared a son who wants to sell women's panties.'

'Selling women's panties would be better than killing myself down the pit.'

'Better? What's good enough for me and your brother isn't good enough for you?'

'That's right Dad, it's not.'

His father was shouting now. 'Footballer, is it? You'll break your bloody neck in those scrums and I'll have to keep you for the rest of your life.'

Tammy's red hair bristled. 'I wouldn't ask you to keep me. I'd never bludge on you.'

'You're bludging on me now. Get a job and pay your way.'

Tammy had enough. Without another word he left the table.

Behind him, his father was still shouting. 'Come back here, you ungrateful bloody lout. Don't you walk away when I'm speaking.'

Tammy was putting clothes into a battered suitcase when his brother came into the room they shared. 'Tammy, what are you doing?'

'The old man said I was bludging on him. I'm not going to cop that. I'm getting out of here.' Tammy slammed the suitcase lid closed.

'You're only sixteen.'

'Old enough to get a job. He said so.'

'He's had too much to drink. We can't have the family break up over some silly comment the old man's made.'

'If I stay under this roof, I'll finish up doing what he wants and go down the pit. That's not for me.' Tammy picked up the suitcase and went out the door.

His first move was to let Norm Bailey know he'd cleared out from home. Bailey, owner of the town's only department store, was the rugby league team's manager and benefactor.

When he answered the knock on the door and saw Tammy with a suitcase, he frowned. 'Don't tell me you're going on holidays. We need you for Saturday.'

'No holiday, Mr Bailey. I've left home.'

'You're not leaving town, are you? The team can't do without you.'

'I don't want to leave town, but I'll have to if I can't find a job.'

'Come inside, my boy,' Bailey said. 'We can talk better in there.'

He ushered the boy into the house and listened while Tammy told of the family argument that caused him to leave home.

Bailey made sympathetic noises. 'I can't solve your problem with your dad but you have two other problems—you have to find a job and somewhere to live.'

Tammy shrugged. 'I haven't had time to think about it.'

'How do you feel about coming to work for me at the store and moving in here in the spare room?'

Tammy whooped with joy. 'Gee, Mr Bailey, I've only been gone from home ten minutes and I've got a job and somewhere to live.'

The floor manager at the store, told by Bailey to give the boy whatever he wanted, raised surprised eyebrows when he wanted to work in the department that sold women's panties.

Tammy didn't really want to be selling women's panties—he wanted his father to hear the sort of work he was doing.

Bailey saw to it that Tammy had all the time off he needed for football training. The boy's game benefited and nobody was surprised when he was selected in the Country side to play City—an annual match in Sydney that gave the best players in the state an opportunity to show ability that could lead to lucrative contracts.

Tammy's brilliant debut made the headlines. A city club quickly had a pen in his hand, signing him for a fee that took his breath away.

In his first year as a professional, Tammy was selected for City. The following year he made the State squad. Many were predicting he'd soon be among the youngest ever to wear the green-and-gold of his country.

George Meetson and his father crouched in the black dust of the skip. The pit pony was sliding on its haunches to hold back the string of wagons on the tunnel's steep incline. Above their heads the craggy roof, so close they could touch it, had dark water seeping through moss-edged cracks. The rails the skips ran on disappeared into the black void ahead.

On either side, a line of thin saplings could be the bald trunks of trees in a leafless forest in hell. The heat was intense. The air the men breathed was laced with coal dust. The flickering light from their carbide lamps created dancing silhouettes on the black walls. The lamps' spluttering naked flames could touch off a gas explosion that could kill them and everyone in the mine, but it was all they had to see by.

At the pit's bottom, the two men left the skip and walked to the dark cave that was their workplace. They put their crib out of the reach of the pit rats, hung their flannel shirts on a pit prop and, naked to the waist, started shovelling coal into a skip. The seam was too low for them to straighten their backs. Soon, their tortured muscles were aching and sweat was coursing down their bodies, creating white rivulets in the coal dust that covered them.

When they needed more coal to fill, they drilled holes in the seam, gently tamped in gelignite and detonators, lit the fuses and scampered for cover.

Before returning to the coalface, they made sure no shots had misfired.

It was then they heard a creaking noise that sounded like a rusty hinge that needed oil. Cracks appeared in the low roof above their heads, zig-zagging in a crazy pattern.

Charlie had seen such cracks before. 'Go for your life, boy,' he yelled. 'The roof's coming down.'

Before they could move, an avalanche of coal and stone buried them.

Tammy was at training when word came that his father and brother were trapped by a mine cave-in. He borrowed a car and covered the distance to the mine at reckless speed.

When he skidded to a stop, rescuers in breathing apparatus were entering the cage to go down below. He tried to jump in with them but the rescue brigade chief held him back. 'You can't go down, son, without oxygen and protective gear. It's a hell of a mess—there could be poisonous gas and the roof could come down again.'

Tammy pushed the restraining hand away. 'I'm going down. It's my dad and brother.'

He was in the cage when it descended into the depths.

Down there, dust was still rising from the mountain of stone and coal that was burying George and Charlie Meetson. When Tammy heard faint sounds that indicated the men were alive, he went into a frenzy, throwing aside huge slabs he normally couldn't lift. Beside him the mines rescue men worked feverishly.

Much of the pile had been cleared and the trapped men were close to being freed when the roof began an ominous creaking.

'Out of here,' the rescue brigade chief roared. 'It's coming down again.'

His men scurried back to safety but Tammy stayed, throwing aside coal and shale. He was still there when the roof thundered down and a huge slab of stone pinned both his legs. Before he lost consciousness, through the mist of pain, he could see white bone poking through the skin.

When the dust settled and the roof seemed more stable, the rescuers went back to where Tammy was alive but mercifully still unconscious. Somehow the roof cave-in had smashed only his legs. It took the combined strength of several rescuers to lift the slab off him.

He was carried to the surface and a waiting ambulance took him to hospital. There, medical staff, undecided at first whether to amputate both crushed legs, managed to save them. But Tammy would never walk again.

Further attempts to save his father and brother were called off because of more falls. The unstable roof forced safety authorities to declare this section of the mine too dangerous to enter. It was closed permanently, never to be worked again.

The heap of coal and shale became the tomb of George and Charlie Meetson. They were left there, buried forever.

Buried with them were Tammy Meetson's footballing dreams.

The Visit

Morna Seres

On the afternoon Holly had agreed to meet David, it was raining. Her eyes followed thick and slippery water streaming down the windows of the Uber, draping the car in heavy sheets, thorough and unpretentious. Pressing her hand against the glass, she wished for the hundredth time she hadn't said yes to David and that she was at home with a drink in her hand and her feet on the couch.

The driver stopped fifty metres short of her destination.

'It's another block,' she said.

'They closed the street, luv.'

She got out of the car at the same time as she tried to negotiate her umbrella. The puddles were deep as she crossed the street towards the newly paved mall and, as she picked up her feet carefully, a car went past and muddy water rose over her shoes. People were hurrying by in plastic skins, umbrellas flying inside out. A man, already soaked, ran by with a hand above his head as if that might protect him. Because her raincoat was flapping about, she pulled it close around her. It seemed as if the fledgling trees lining the mall might be ripped from the ground, the wind was so fierce.

Outside the bar, her foot slipped out of her shoe and she fell hard onto her hip. As she hit the pavement, she let go of her suede handbag and now the lower half was stained with water marks. Standing unsteadily, she walked up the steps, trying to compose herself.

Moving through the entrance, someone shouted, 'Shut the bloody door, will you?' She looked over to see who it was and saw a man bulging out of his suit, his neck thick and lined. Ignoring him, she looked around and saw David sitting at a table near the window at the back of the bar. It was strange to get a view of him before he'd noticed her. She realised she'd forgotten he was almost ugly. Ugly beautiful with his big nose and classic jawline. He was wearing a thick leather jacket even though it was humid. Making her way towards him, the air smelt of soggy coats and women's perfume.

He stood as soon as he saw her and she couldn't quite believe he was really there; it had been over sixteen years since she'd seen him. Leaning over, he kissed her on both cheeks. 'How are you, Hols?'

'Wet,' she said, taking off her raincoat and shaking out her hair, worrying she didn't look at all the way she had when she'd left the house. He had flown in from a summer in Italy and his skin was golden. The hair on his head reached down past his collar, a fringe fell across his eyes.

He put his arm up to summon a waiter. 'Martini with a twist?'

'You remember.'

'Of course.'

'When did you get in?'

'This morning. Terrible flight, we bounced the whole way.'

Looking across the room, she observed the barman pouring a beer, tipping the glass and throwing off the froth. The place was crowded, three deep where people were ordering, and the music sounded loud and unfamiliar.

'The waiter seems to be ignoring us,' she said.

'I can't imagine anyone ignoring you.'

She mustered a smile. 'Aren't you hot? In your coat?'

He shrugged himself out of his jacket and she looked past him, out the window at the falling light and the endless patter of rain. When he was back with her, she noticed how haggard his face had become.

'You're alright?' she asked.

He smiled. She'd forgotten how pretty he was when he did that, his teeth even and white.

'A few creaky joints,' he said. 'You look exactly the same. Better.'

She looked down at the wooden table. It appeared to be newly lacquered and shone brightly under the low lights. 'It was a surprise. Getting your call after all these years,' she said. It seemed as though he was getting ready to say something, so she quickly said, 'How's Jenny?'

'She died.'

'Oh no. I'm so sorry, I had no idea. What happened?'

'Cancer.' He tried again to get the waiter's attention. 'I think you're right, he is ignoring us.'

'When?'

'Nearly four years. A while now.'

'I suppose it is.' Sophie, her daughter, would have been just twelve, in her first year of high school.

'And Ben? How is he?'

'They forced him into an early retirement.'

'I'm sorry to hear that.' He looked at her directly and it sent a charge through her. 'I still think of you,' he said, his voice low and gravelly.

She looked down at his hands, slim and brown, the gold band still on his ring finger.

'This downpour was a surprise,' she said. 'The sun was out and I thought, no, it's not going to rain, even though they said it would. But I was wrong and those weather people were right for a change.'

'Italy was so dry when I left.'

Holly remembered how green it was over there. Jenny had told her once it was because it rained all winter. The year she and Ben had visited it had been unbearably hot, the air crackling. She recalled clumps of trees across hills and down in the valleys, terracotta villas dotting the hillsides like the one where David and Jenny lived. The four of them had spent afternoons lying around the pool, baking under a burning sun. At nine each morning, they'd gone in the car to a village where they drank strong coffee and ate sweet pastries. Some days, they walked through forests where branches hung low and light sprinkled onto the ground in patches like rain drops. On one particular day, she caught David looking at her. It was the first time she had an inkling of where things were heading.

But remembering those times wasn't helpful. Until David had phoned, she'd mostly managed to rid herself of their past.

'How are the boys?' she asked.

'They're at university in Milan. It seems like it was only yesterday when they were running around with your lot. They must be grown too.'

'They've left home. At least the boys have. Sophie, of course, is still at school.' She looked over her shoulder. The place was heaving. 'Is there any chance you could get the waiter's attention? I really could do with that drink.'

'Do you remember the night we were so drunk we let off firecrackers and the cypress tree near the front of the house caught fire. You ran off.

You were so frightened and I had to find you.'

She closed her eyes and said, 'Don't.' And then she felt ridiculous because what she'd said seemed so emotionally heavy and her eyes were welling up.

He reached into his pocket. 'Hey, darling, don't cry. Here, I've got a hanky.'

'Do people still carry those around?' she said, as she took it.

'I'm not lying when I say I think about you.'

It was getting dark outside and a streetlight went on.

'Ben doesn't know I'm here,' she said.

He nodded. 'What about Sophie?'

Holly had been waiting for this and it was sad and embarrassing all at the same time. 'It would have been so much better if you hadn't come,' she said.

'I've wanted to see you for so long.'

'Stop.' She straightened herself.

'What is she like?' he asked.

Holly drew a breath deep into her lungs and let it go. 'She's...she's lovely. Bright...bright and happy. She's...light, you know, optimistic.'

'Like you.'

'God no, she's like...I'm sorry...do you think you deserve this?'

He didn't say anything for a time, so she said, 'I can't believe that happened to Jenny, of all people.'

'We buried her on that hill, the one near the church you loved.'

'She was so vibrant, so capable.'

'Yes, she was all of that.' He came in close, close enough she could smell his skin. 'I missed you,' he said. 'For a long time. Terribly on certain days.'

She looked out the window, unsure how to consider this. The storm had died down and there was a break between the clouds. She could see stars against a black sky, the wet mall shimmering under the light. 'It's beautiful out there,' she said. 'Like a set for a Hollywood movie.'

'Does she know about me?'

The scene felt tawdry suddenly, overly dramatic, and still she couldn't help herself. 'You said you'd come back. You said you were going to sort it out. And I waited for months. Not even an email or a phone call.'

Two men walking past the window stopped. She noticed because one of the men pushed the other one roughly against the shoulder. A few seconds later, they came through the door and sat down at the table beside her.

'It wasn't because I didn't love you,' David said.

'You have to stop this.'

'Can't I explain?'

'No.'

'I never stopped loving you.'

She looked up quickly. 'But you stayed with her.'

For a while, neither of them said anything. In the silence, it was hard not to notice the two men at the next table raising their voices. One of them said, 'You're a fucking liar,' loud enough that several people in the room looked over.

David put his hand over hers. 'I'd like to see Sophie. I came to see you both.'

Shaking her head, 'None of this is making any sense. Being here today and seeing you. It's all jumbled up, like it's the collapse of something.'

'Please, I need to see her.'

She withdrew her hand. She'd had enough of the conversation. She could only think of crawling into bed. A sudden movement beside them took her by surprise. The two men were on their feet, hitting one another, and the thwacking sound of fists butting up against bone and breaking skin was awful and incomprehensible. Both she and David jumped back and pushed themselves against the window as blood and mucous flew across the room. Things happened very quickly after that. There was a lot of screaming and shouting as the waiter and barman rushed over, separating the men. Eventually they left, yelling obscenities at everyone in the bar.

Holly realised she and David were clutching on to one another. Despite the horror of the fight, she felt oddly invigorated and fought a surprising impulse to laugh. When they sat down again, the street lamp lit one side of his face and, as he started to cry, she remembered how sentimental he could be. She tried to understand what the two of them were to each other, but their history was limited, a collection of fragments that had at times been explosive and, at other times, remarkably tender.

Holly sensed that to anyone looking at them, they might seem sad. It made her sad. What was she so frightened of? They were nothing in the end but a transitory collection of living cells. None of this would mean anything after they were gone. The anger that had quietly gnawed at her for years deserted her.

She took a photo out of her bag and handed it to him. 'She reads books, lots of them. She told me the other day she wants to study literature when she leaves school.'

His face lost that hurt look and he smiled, tracing the image with his finger. 'She looks like you,' he said.

'People say that.' She picked up her coat. 'We didn't lie about you. Ben insisted she know.' Holly stood up.

'No. Don't go. Look, the waiter's coming.'

Holly paused. The weather had cleared and the full moon was a round fist of white ice, a blazing ball lighting up silhouetted buildings along the mall.

Roundabout

Lisa Kate Moule

Mandy went to a high school on the outskirts of the suburbs, solidly inland but named Whittlesea. The school stood amongst a small cluster of shops on the main road. A nursery with attention-grabbing signage but almost nothing out the back, a McDonalds and a small park with a children's roundabout that squealed at night in the wind.

The school had a permanent air of neglect. A frill of dandelions and milky thistles skirted the concrete blocks and beaten up portables; there were no boasting lawns or manicured gardens. The reception held stuffy cabinets with the school uniform displayed on headless mannequins, and very outdated needlework by students who had left to early pregnancies. The ground was hard, impacted like rock, which turned to mud in the rain.

Crows sat like rotten fruit in far off trees and swept in at the end of lunch for scraps. Filthy footfall lay stamped over hallways, left a violated undertone in its emptiness when class began.

The fighting was healthy; the tempers, the rage and the anger management issues were the routine that the curriculum interrupted occasionally. The teachers were taking each day at a time, breathing deeply, often 'never-coming-back'. Sometimes, a class from hell could unite over the sport of a young, new teacher—you can't send the whole class out. A lot of those young teachers never made it to lunchtime.

Mandy and her two friends, Brooke and Kelly, wore blue eyeliner and hip-high skirts and would coast off to the toilets and smoke during class.

Mandy's year eight science teacher's shirts were threadbare and his hair was full of long wisps and flaps. His voice was hoarse from overpowering every class. When students got out of hand, he'd turn red shouting 'in my office,' his spittle spraying into the air. They would all laugh about what his wife might look like.

Mandy developed enemies so close to friends she couldn't weed out the difference. At night, great hypothetical comeback lines would keep her awake. If someone fought her with flair, she liked them more.

The headmistress said, 'Sit down ladies. I use the term loosely.' The condescension was clear; it kept her temper alight.

Sometime in year nine, it became cool not to know the answers to school work. 'I don't fuck'n know,' she'd say aloud in class. It got a laugh. 'Dumb slut,' said one of the boys. The science teacher pretended not to hear.

She regularly skipped school with Brooke and Kelly. At the mall, they'd prey on other girls from neighbouring schools with the same thick eyeliner and piercings up their ear—a type of needlework you could say—and identical short skirts that made them look unmothered.

Young mothers would censor the direction of their strollers.

Mandy knew how to survive; it had nothing to do with school. There's no probability, or history of Ancient Rome, or irony in real life. Although, the mall was called the Forum and the graffiti artists (volunteers) would always out-work the cleaners (paid).

News travelled fast in Whittlesea. Word got out that the rich girl, Jen's, parents—the girl with the tennis court and pool—were away for the weekend, and she was having a few people around. At the party, they danced, drank coolers and laughed-their-heads-off at Jen's family portraits. She saw the fear in Jen's eyes as she failed to close the door against crowds of alien teenagers from schools in the next town. Crowds built on the nature strip.

Unfamiliar boys flipped the kitchen table over, threw Kraft cheese slices in the fish tank and pushed girls in the pool.

A gang with a ghetto blaster of dense, overpowering music forced their way in. One of the boys, who had an unsettled look—whose thoughts didn't sit neatly inside his body—broke a chair leg on Brooke's toe.

'Who the fuck're you?' said Mandy and tipped the cutlery draw over his head when he bent down to turn up the ghetto blaster. Everyone laughed. He grabbed a steak knife from the floor among the silver and stabbed it into the parquet, millimeters from Mandy's shoe. Anyone she recognised disappeared. She was frozen with fear. She willed herself to leave at that moment. She would wish that for a long time after, when it played back in her head.

The boy's face had changed when she looked back at him. There were no specific expressions, no movements of features, no smile; just a gradual filling of energy in his face, like he'd been plugged in. Mandy's heart was thumping into her ears.

Unknown hands ripped at her crop top. She was covering up her breasts with her hands when she heard a loud crack and realised it was the sound of her head smacking the kitchen floor, her back suddenly cold.

She was dragged, pulled by her hair, to the adjoining laundry with a sliding door. A hand over her throat, her head against the washing machine. The pain in her head swelled to a peak when a dirty tea towel was pulled tight over her face.

Bodies crushed her. Her chest tight. Her lungs not able to fill, struggling for breath. They forced their way in. Pain between her legs that happened so quickly but never seemed to end. Permanently stealing her from herself.

The sliding door opened. Someone shouted, 'Get off her, you fuck'n arseholes, the cops are here.'

She told no one about what had happened. Not even her friends, not her mother either. In the aftermath she blamed herself, her mother probably would anyway.

Two senior officers asked about Mandy's qualifications as they glanced through her CV on the desk between them. She mirrored their interlaced fingers. Their exteriors were hard, as though crime-fighting had metastasized into a sheen. They'd clearly tucked in any corners of frayed psychology.

The officers listened to her strengths and weaknesses while she crossed her legs to match theirs. Their tight jaws and chins formed a punch. Their speech cadence was an in-house brand where words arrived slowly, protracted, as though their heads were constipated with thoughts too big to pass.

They had a list of questions to tick off before they could draw up a contract.

Including: Are you mentally strong? Would you be able to look at photos of victims' bodies on a regular basis? Have you ever had a mental breakdown?

Near the end of her interview, the important one asked, 'What will you do with your kids?'

Imagine him being asked about his kids in a job interview. 'Oh, thought I'd bring 'em round to yours,' she replied to the Chief of Police.

The female officer, next to him, smirked, gave Mandy a look that said you're in.

The lift full of gold mirrors spilled out onto an enormous vestibule, like a superhero's lair.

A huge circular woven rug, with HQ embroidered on it, pinpointed the forum space where everything met. Stairs spiralled upwards. A reception desk in one long line with five women in headsets all dazzled in concentration.

She was met by Officer Tracey who interviewed her. She greeted Mandy warmly and introduced her to the receptionists. Altogether, in strappy dresses and fruity perfume, they waved in minute gestures. Could tell some of them were still on calls.

Mandy followed her up the stairs, where offices were partitioned off into cubicles overlooking a carpark and the back end of a hotel. Tracey introduced her to colleagues. Their names skidded through her head. Mandy received hand-shakes and smiles, even a wink. Tracey found Mandy a desk, her very own space.

'Here's the kitchen, toilet and that's where the bosses are, upstairs.' Tracey made some very clear and deliberate arm gestures—she'd obviously directed traffic before.

'Oh, here's your welcome pack.' There was a pamphlet titled, 'Equal Opportunity Employers', a lanyard and a memory stick. 'This is how to get into the system…let's have a look. For example, I could type in…a shooting…in say…Brunswick and these would all pop up.' A series of bloody and harrowing images appeared without filtering.

Mandy finally sat down at her desk at 10am. Eyes twitching. Body limp. Computer keys gently clicked around her.

The first three photos were the worst. Three women, frozen in violence. An odd, impossible angle with the right leg. She had to create a casefile, upload the picture, write up the facts, email to relevant people.

She lost her appetite for lunch in the first week. It seemed wholly inappropriate for her to eat a sandwich over these people. 'If you need to speak to someone, you know, we can provide that,' Tracey had said. There was a list of contacts, all on the stick. She still had another 200 to get through before the end of the first day.

She could manage by being at the end of her finger tips as they pressed the button in the lift, marched over computer keys, played with the lanyard around her neck absentmindedly, which immobilised her brain.

Somebody popped their head over into her work space. 'Surviving? Hi, I'm Stewart. It's actually funny—horror has no effect on me whatsoever. I'm just totally desensitised to any gore. It's pretty weird. You'll get there.'

'Oh thanks,' she said. Frozen.

Inbox: a naked woman's body with a towel over her head. Mandy fumbled with the lanyard. She spun the chair away from her desk, braced herself against that feeling like she was going to faint. The fast-paced keyboards clicked around her like a rising tide.

'Oh Mandy,' said Tracey. 'There's a meeting at 11am you need to attend.'

She ran straight to the toilet. Steadied herself against the cubicle wall until her breathing slowed.

Eased back over to her desk and focused on small objects around her. She managed to right herself through details. Hard shoes, pencil holder, mouse, pamphlet, stapler, framed photo of children, keep-cup.

She arrived late to the meeting.

Jokes padded out the job. The Senior Sergeant said, 'Women's problems were a good excuse to get out of meetings…We're just having fun, after you…What about men's rights hey? Ha-ha.'

Maybe she did need that extra help? The counsellor was free to anyone who needed it, and was anonymous. But anyone could see the office, and anyone could see who knocked at the door.

Back at her desk. Everyone stopped working and stood up. A round of applause erupted throughout the entire floor. A strapping guy began to well-up but stopped himself. There was back slapping and bear hugs. Stewart explained to her that the young guy had made a significant arrest after a public shooting. 'You'd betta start watching the news, mate. Not spending all ya time watching *The Bachelor*. Ha-ha.'

When the receptionists began to wear tight woollen knits and long leather boots, Tracey approached Mandy. 'I need you and Stewart to handle this one for me. It's a side-step. Its manning the station all night, up in woop-woop. Don't worry, nothing's happening there, you just have to show up.'

'They've got a Maccas,' said Stewart.

At 3am, a girl entered with a short skirt and a miniscule crop top. Mandy interlaced her fingers on the desk. Stewart rolled his eyes at Mandy as the girl, who was probably fifteen, stumbled in heels at the counter. Her face blurring with runaway make up and a ripped top. She hiccupped.

'Honestly,' said Stewart, as her top gaped open. 'She's begging for trouble.'

Mandy asked her, 'How can we help at this time of the morning?' She spoke slowly, filtering out prejudice, which wasn't easy at this end of the day. Her speech-cadence, the in-house brand, was effective at holding everything in.

'I'd like to report a rape,' said the girl. Her voice broken. Her body shaking.

Mandy crossed her arms. Stewart flexed his jaw and looked at his watch. The roundabout squealed in the wind.

Wonder Lost

Regina Botros

He ran away to the circus. For most people that's a joke, like going out for milk and never coming back. For me, my dad joined a travelling circus. I was eleven so I understood the appeal.

I did visit him once and he was operating the Ferris wheel, it was a bittersweet feeling being able to ride as many times as I wanted. Round and round I'd go, I'm not sure why I got off every time. But I did, joining the non-existent queue to ride again and again.

When he left, there were so many questions, so many gaps in his wake.

I was at an age where days just turn and turn. The monotony of life seemed at its peak and summers were long, stretching endlessly in the blistering heat like bubble gum stuck to your shoe, melting and aimless. I spent many hours lying on my bed, reading sweet sixteen books faster and faster, trying to beat my time to completion, or dancing around the living room with a white scarf pinned to my head, pretending I had long, straight, blonde hair like my little sister.

My dad gave me my first job delivering hot coffee to the big hall of housie players so they didn't miss their numbers; legs eleven, legs eleven, eighteen coming of age, fifty-five snakes alive. The hall was full of focused concentration and I weaved around them light footed and wide eyed taking and delivering their orders. I remember one man with black hair that reached to the floor and thumb nails so thick and long they grew in a spiral, circling around and around. I was mesmerised almost spilling his hot tea all over him.

As I did another round of the Ferris wheel I thought, my dad seemed to fit right in dressed in a blue terry towelling hat, a wife beater singlet and shorts operating this big turning machine. The carny folk were mostly sweaty men, a kind of subgroup of society. I couldn't help wondering how he got this job, was it passing through town and last minute he decided to join the troupe? Was it something he always wanted to do? I wondered if he'd get me a job there too. I hoped so.

His leaving sent my life into a kind of death roll, the collateral damage of his actions, ricocheting for years to come.

I was in my wonder years. It was the suburbs and we had a standard house that was extended on. There was a trampoline and a sand pit, a cockatoo that swore, chickens with eggs to be collected, a goat and ducks, and a small garden of vegetables we had to pick or peel depending on the season. There was a plum tree bearing fruit and a mulberry tree that offered silkworms for me to keep in an ice cream container in a cupboard, watching them spin their silk over weeks and months till they emerged, transformed.

We lived a couple of blocks away from my cousins and we raced our bikes around the block and played 'Doctors and Nurses' in the back shed which had a pin up calendar on the door with a different half-naked woman for each month. We put on dance shows for the family and sold homemade cards to neighbours for 20c and 50c. I smoked my first cigarette under the house next door with the neighbour, a Winnie blue I stole from my dad's packet. Strangely, I don't remember the neighbour who joined me in this initiation, but I remember their mother, Cheryl, who became my mum's friend when my dad left. She was married to a sailor who went away for months at a time. They drank coffee often. She seemed exciting and bohemian and commented on my great calf muscles, as if drawing out the woman in me.

That women even considered how their calves looked was a marvel, I began to see myself differently, walking on my toes imagining high heels and skirts that showed them to their best vantage.

That fateful day started like any other. Up early, my mum brushing my curly locks into a frizzy pony tail while I watched thunderbirds and walking my little sister to school, it was my last year of primary school and her first. It's funny to think about the moments before a big event, the before times. The innocence seems almost embarrassingly naïve. That afternoon, became the after times.

Stunned, it was like emerging from a dark cave into a new reality where nothing is familiar and the brightness is hard to adjust your eyes to. You know something important is happening but you're not sure what it means. There's a sense of something unusual in the air and a kind of dull shock descended on our house. Time slowed, like if we stayed as close to the event in time maybe everything will catch up. But the further away it becomes, the less likely things will return to before and everything rushed away like the wave leaving the shore.

Left in his wake was a list of unanswered questions; where was he? Was he OK? What could have happened? Did he just forget to come home? Vacancy.

My future was interrupted. Mum decided we had to move house which was devastating for me. I was supposed to start high school with my cousins and I was supposed to teach at the dance school I'd been at since I was four. I had almost completed my Royal Academy of Dance training and had a job lined up to teach at the new dance school my teacher was opening. I could do nearly ten pirouettes in point shoes in a row–you had to spot a mark otherwise you'd lose your balance. My mark moved and I lost my balance.

It was like I was on the Ferris wheel but something shifted and I was forced to ride the Ghost Train. I don't really like things that intentionally try to scare you; it was just fine going around and around watching the small people below. The ride stopped at the top of the circle. The men at the circus looked tired and vacant and I knew then it must not be as much fun for them as it was for me, their life had beaten the wonder out of them. Like finally making it to Oz only to find the magic is a man behind a curtain operating a big machine that makes things appear more wonderful than they are.

In our new home, we–my mother, my sister and me–started going to social dancing every Monday. I was very good at it and joined the competitive team. It was very *Strictly Ballroom*. I started looking forward to it more and more because there was a boy at the classes. He was also a very good dancer and sometimes called the rounds in square dancing. There are a number of different sequences you can do and the caller sends partners do-si-do-ing and weaving all around the floor in this patterned dance. It's called square dancing, but it's more circular, spinning partners around and around.

This boy started turning up out of the blue at my house. It was exciting and strange. I'd wait at the window for him to come and pick me up to take me to class or to a movie. Until one afternoon, after school, we had our first kiss in the hallway of this new house. I had a boyfriend.

He started staying over more and more, sleeping in the living room, mostly. He was older than me, five years older and I was thirteen by now. I didn't want the same things as him. I wanted to write love letters of longing. He wanted to see what was under my skirt. I wanted to practice our dance moves. He wanted to practice different kinds of moves. He said he wanted to marry me. I said I'm too young. He said please a lot, I said no a lot. He said if you love me then, I said ok a few times, but felt like saying no all the time. He sometimes didn't ask, and I woke up sometimes to find it was too late to say no.

It was around this time that Dad started showing up again. He was back. He loved us. He started living with us and got a job and life was back to a new normal. He came to dance nights with us and he took back his chair at the dining table and his chair in the living room. Was it a week? Was it several months, a year? The inconsequence of time at the time prevailed and then he didn't come home, again. It was less surprising.

But, I was optimistic, I told my mum that he'd probably come back. And I am not sure if she thought I was ready to know the truth, if I should wake up, or that she was so hurt she felt the only way I would realise was if she showed me the letter. A letter that told us it was over and that he had found another woman, another family that he loved, and that he wouldn't be coming back and that he didn't love us anymore. I saw the man in terry towelling operating a big machine that promised magic but delivered reality.

The Ferris wheel stopped and I got off. I was given a ticket to the show in the big top. I walked past the clowns with their slowly shaking heads like I'd done something wrong, open mouthed and tempting you with the chance of a fluffy toy to take home. I really wanted one of those fluffy toys.

In the big top, I sat alone. Was Mum talking with Dad about us, trying to convince him to come home while I sat watching trapeze acts, juggling clowns, and prancing horses with monkeys on their backs? I wondered if he got to sleep in a caravan, I hoped so and was dying to see it.

What I didn't know at the time was that my father was an alcoholic and a gambler; he used to leave my little sister in the car for hours with the window cracked while he gambled at the local TAB and drank in the adjoining pub. I didn't know that he gambled our house away, leaving my mother with his debt, forcing us to sell and move again and again till she had nothing left to sell. And I didn't know that he wasn't my biological father, and that my father was, in fact, Egyptian with curly brown hair just

187

like me, and that he left when I was two years old. Dull shock. We moved. Again.

I told my boyfriend I couldn't marry him and we broke up. I changed schools, again. I stopped dancing altogether and everything turned in a new direction.

As I left the circus, that sweltering day, I walked past the animals; the elephants that were being washed after their hard work carrying acrobats on their backs, and the lions lying in their small cages, sleeping in the heat. I thought it would be great to work here; still hoping my dad would get me a job. I thought it'd be wonderful to be so close to the magic, to live inside it every day.

He gave me a huge stuffed animal and one to take home for my little sister, his biological daughter. I said goodbye to him and promised to visit again.

Did he notice that I never came back?